PRAISE FOR *Bo...*

"[*Born into This* is] a potent collection by an author who mined the richness of both his ancestry, his work within the Aboriginal community and his island home for tales about black and white relations, colonialism, class friction, racism and the despoilment of heritage and environment... With its wit, intelligence and restless exploration of the parameters of race and place, Thompson's debut collection is a welcome addition to the canon of Indigenous Australian writers."
—THUY ON, *THE GUARDIAN*

"[A] riveting debut collection. Stories of brutal weather and angry bees, urban protests and remote islands, trace the tether between Tasmanian Aboriginal people and their ancestral lands. Thompson's strengths are in his exquisite descriptions of nature, as well as his memorable voice."
—*PUBLISHERS WEEKLY*

"A short story collection reminiscent of the work of Black American author Edward P. Jones... These stories are touching precisely because they are so familiar. That they tell the stories of people from Australia makes no difference. People realize the need to find ways to reclaim their histories. Through agriculture, by storytelling, through activism, and most importantly by living free lives. Thompson shows us how artfully."
—DONNA LEDBETTER, SHORT STORY BOOK CLUB

"The Tasmanian landscape and a whole host of engaging, charming and well drawn characters populate the stories that make up *Born Into This*... a wonderful reminder that there is no monolithic Aboriginal Australian... a thought provoking collection, and hopefully a conversation provoking collection too."
—SIMON CLARK, *THE AU REVIEW*

"*Born Into This* includes a range of stories that highlight the racism and oppression that many different First Nations people face in our current day, while also making the reader pause and think about the reality of these fictional stories... It is a stunning collection from a talented and compelling debut author. Thompson has given Australia a new voice to listen to and learn from in 2021."
—LAUREN PRATT, *UNDERGROUND WRITERS*

"Some stories are morbidly comic while others cut deep, conveying the absurdity and despair of Indigenous experiences of settler-colonialism across Tasmania."
—TRISTEN HARWOOD, *THE SATURDAY PAPER*

"This collection of Indigenous resistance, triumph and joy stands alongside millions of stories throughout this country, first spoken, then written, since time immemorial."
—RAVEENA GROVER, *KILL YOUR DARLINGS*

"This remarkable debut crackles with wit and rage — as entertaining and affecting as it is thought-provoking."
—STELLA CHARLS, *READINGS*

"A new collection of short stories addresses the universal themes of identity, racism and heritage destruction."
—DANA ANDERSON, *THE EXAMINER*

"With *Born into This*, Adam Thompson's stories of present-day Tasmania provide a powerful response to trauma that dates from the horrors of the Black War and continues with ongoing 'celebrations' of Australia/Invasion Day. The author has much to say."
—ANTHONY LYNCH, *AUSTRALIAN BOOK REVIEW*

"*Born Into This* represents the emergence of a fresh and vital voice on the Australian literary scene. Indigenous writer Adam Thompson expertly combines wit and pathos in his debut short story collection. With stories from a diversity of perspectives, but bound by its Tasmanian setting, Thompson's mastery over his characters and sensibility for contemporary issues makes this a special collection."
—*HAPPY MAG*, BEST NEW BOOKS OF 2021

"Piercing. At times funny. Real. Raw. Straight up truth. Stories that urge the reader to reflect, to look inward... This book is a gift."
—BLACKFULLA BOOKCLUB (INSTAGRAM)

"It's beautiful to read such intimate and familiar representations of lutruwita — a place too often rendered as haunting and gothic in the history of Australian literature. These stories cover themes of family, activism, intimacy and identity. I know it's going to be one of those books that is read really widely for years to come."
—EVELYN ARALUEN, AUTHOR OF *DROPBEAR*

"It's not often a new literary voice seems to spring full formed from a world so unique and yet so achingly recognisable, and it's a voice with its own gravitas and unique vision. A debut collection that leaps from the starter's gate."
—CATE KENNEDY, AUTHOR OF *THE WORLD BENEATH*

"I knew from the first page that *Born Into This* was going to be something special. Adam Thompson is a world-class writer whose stories strike like lightning."
—ELLEN VAN NEERVEN, AUTHOR OF *HEAT AND LIGHT*

"The lives of the characters within these pages provide an honest, humorous and occasionally raw insight into the experiences of living in a country, and on Country, both shared and in contest. Thompson is a writer who knows that the way to our hearts and heads is through powerful storytelling. He delivers on every page, with each word."
—**TONY BIRCH, AUTHOR OF *THE WHITE GIRL***

"A compelling new voice, tough yet tender, from the heart of Aboriginal Tasmania."
—**MELISSA LUCASHENKO, AUTHOR OF *TOO MUCH LIP***

"Adam Thompson's stories from Aboriginal Tasmania are as beautifully written as they are evocative. Here is an outstanding new talent. *Born Into This* is compelling reading."
—**BOB BROWN, AUTHOR OF *MEMO FOR A SANER WORLD***

"*Born Into This* is drenched in swagger and originality, the blows are head-on, but the comfort is swiftly delivered in the wit and delicacy of Thompson's phrasing. He has the reader in the boat, on the shore and drowning in the sea at once."
—**TARA JUNE WINCH, AUTHOR OF *THE YIELD***

BORN INTO THIS

STORIES

Adam Thompson

Two Dollar Radio
Books Too loud To Ignore

Two Dollar Radio
Books too loud to Ignore

WHO WE ARE TWO DOLLAR RADIO is a family-run outfit dedicated to reaffirming the cultural and artistic spirit of the publishing industry. We aim to do this by presenting bold works of literary merit, each book, individually and collectively, providing a sonic progression that we believe to be too loud to ignore.

TwoDollarRadio.com

Proudly based in
Columbus
OHIO

 @TwoDollarRadio

 @TwoDollarRadio

 /TwoDollarRadio

Printed in Canada

Love the
PLANET?
So do we.

Printed on Rolland Enviro.
This paper contains 100% post-consumer fiber, is manufactured using renewable energy - Biogas and processed chlorine free.

 100%

PCF

BIO GAS° ENERGY

∞ PERMANENT

All Rights Reserved : COPYRIGHT→ © 2021 BY ADAM THOMPSON

ISBN→ 9781953387042 : *Library of Congress Control Number available upon request.*

Also available as an Ebook.
E-ISBN→ 9781953387059

Book Club & Reader Guide of questions and topics for discussion is available at twodollarradio.com

First published 2021 by University of Queensland Press, Australia

Aboriginal language in this book is palawa kani—the language of Tasmanian Aborigines.

SOME RECOMMENDED LOCATIONS FOR READING *BORN INTO THIS*:
Pretty much anywhere because books are portable and the perfect technology!

AUTHOR PHOTO→
Ness Vanderburgh

COVER AND INTERNAL ART→
Solidarity by
Judith-Rose Thomas

ANYTHING ELSE? Yes. Do not copy this book—with the exception of quotes used in critical essays and reviews—without the prior written permission from the copyright holder and publisher. Without limiting the rights under copyright reserved above, no part of this publication may be reproduced, stored or introduced into a retrieval system, or transmitted, in any form or by any means. **WE MUST ALSO POINT OUT THAT THIS IS A WORK OF FICTION.** Any resemblances to names, places, incidents, or persons, living or dead, are entirely coincidental or are used fictitiously.

In memory of my beautiful and loving mother,
Deidre Jean Anderson
'Dee'
(1957–2008)

CONTENTS

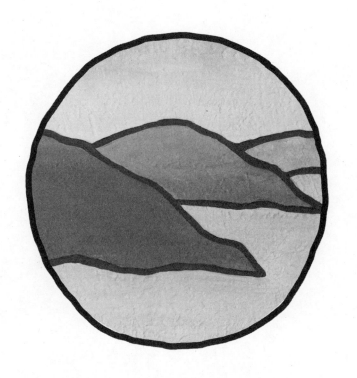

BORN INTO THIS

THE OLD TIN MINE

It wasn't my first survival camp. But when I struck at the damp flint and gouged another piece of flesh out of my knuckle, I swore it would be the last.

'Fucking ... cheap ... rubbish.'

Standing too quickly, I stumbled backward, knocking one of the boys over in the process. He fell, sprawling onto the black sand like a four-legged spider. Kneeling too long by the fire had locked up my knees. Old knees. *Too old for this shit.*

'I'll have a go if you like, Ben?' Chris took my spot next to the small teepee of sticks I'd stuffed with the driest bracken fern I could find. He took up the flint. I turned my back on them and made out I was checking my phone. Inside my pocket, I formed a tight fist, squeezing the pain out of my throbbing hand.

'I've already done most of the fucking work anyway,' I said over my shoulder.

From the sound of shuffling feet and heightened positivity in the chatter, I figured Chris was having some success with the fire. Looking for somewhere to rest, I sought out his pack amongst those dumped in the middle of our camping spot and sat down on it, hard. Something gave under my weight, followed by a muffled tinkle of glass.

Fuck him. Raytji has no business out here with us anyway.

I looked over when I heard the boys cooing at the first puffs of smoke.

'There we go, lads,' said Chris. 'Just remember what Uncle Ben showed you about making a fire. It can mean the difference between staying comfy and warm and being cold and miserable. Right?'

'Not to mention being able to eat something now,' added Jacob, the eldest of the boys. He had assumed the alpha role amongst the others — aided by the accounts of how many guys he'd 'smashed' recently — while we'd waited for the Cessna at the dusty airstrip.

The boys stretched their hands toward the newborn flame as it reluctantly drew up into the apex of the sticks, teasing at warmth. There were six of them. Aboriginal teens. City boys. Three from Launceston, three from Hobart. *Fair split, north and south*, according to the organization that had won the black money.

'As long as they're true mob, I don't care where they're from,' I'd said, when the two in charge made contact. 'But it's fifteen hundred a day and you supply the gear. Take it or leave it.' I'd shrugged as they eyeballed each other, like a husband and wife after opening the winter power bill. But, in this case, there was nobody to pin the blame on for overusing the clothes dryer or running a fridge in the garage. This was specialized work. And who else was going to do the job? Sure, there were other black-fellas in the game. But these people would ask around — white-fellas always did. *Consulting the community*, they called it. What it would come down to was reliability — in their eyes anyway. And I'd been getting the lion's share of the heritage work for years. Plus, this group had been sitting on the money for a while. That was on the public record. *Aboriginal survival camp — Clarke Island*. State government grant from the previous year. With the acquittal looming, they had to roll it out, and they needed someone. Quick.

When the letter arrived saying, *Congratulations*, I slapped my side. *Piss weak*. Fancy taking your hat off to someone holding you over a barrel like that. They did throw in a catch, though, and insisted on one of *their* people going along.

'Occupational health and safety,' they said. 'Can't avoid it nowadays.' Chris Foster, their man, had all the certification, and a goddamned 'Working with Children' card too. I almost pulled out, but jobs like this were my bread and butter — and they were getting more and more infrequent.

~

'You fellas want to get some firewood together, ay.' The boys were still huddled around the fire. 'Don't just stand around. Lance, you're helping me with dinner tonight. Over here, matey, please.'

Lance left the fire and rummaged through some of the bags half-heartedly.

'Can't find the abalone, Uncle Ben.'

'Fuck off, you can't?'

The boys turned at my raised voice.

'I told you fellas to grab 'em, didn't I?' I pointed to each one in turn. 'Don't tell me youse left 'em back on that beach?'

'All good. They're in my pack,' said Chris, coming to the rescue again, like the white knight he was. I visualized myself punching him to the ground.

He placed the bundle of sticks he had gathered next to the fire and hurried over to his pack. 'Umm, Ben, I'm sorry, but I think you're sitting on my bag … I'll just get the abs out, if that's all right.'

'Cheers, matey,' I said, standing. The dry grind of arthritis made my movement jagged and slow. I raised my voice again so they could all hear. 'You boys wanna remember: this is about survival. We're blackfellas. We've survived for thousands of bloody years in the bush — without the need for any of this shit.' I threw an accusing finger at the pile of bags and then let it linger on Chris, who had his back to the group. 'Now, help Lance get them abs ready and we'll cook 'em when I get back.'

'Knee still sore?' asked Chris, in a sympathetic tone. He was rummaging through his bag. 'There's some wrap in the kit, if you think that would help … Oh, bugger, looks like my lamp is broken.'

'Just chuck us a shit roll, will ya?' I said.

~

I rolled a joint after that, by the light of my head torch. I held on to each puff for as long as I could. *Maximum benefit* was a strong motto I lived by. So was *work smart, not hard.* And so the heritage game suited me: archaeological work, surveys, guiding. The work came in blocks but paid very well. And it was nearly always remote, so on top of the pay came allowances and accommodation. The money was good — great, in fact. But you had to make what you got last, even in the face of abundance. I wasn't like some of our other mob in the game: two-bob millionaires while the coin was rolling in but who had Centrelink on speed dial for when the work dried up. I ran my thumb over the crumpled lid of the old spark-plug tin I kept my dope in. We were two days into the camp, and it was still pretty much packed.

Fucking ripper.

Of course, the old 'drug-and-alcohol free' bullshit applied — the usual thing. It was supposed to apply to everyone. But, in my eyes, that rule was for the young fellas — and Chris. I was supposed to be the role model. 'Uncle Ben,' they called me. I've never referred to myself as that, though. The way I was brought up, the status of Elder was given by those who respected you. The self-appointed ones either had something to prove or something to gain.

I'd been smoking weed for most of the forty-two years since the family moved to town in '77, and no prick — black, white or brindle — was ever going to stop me. But, of course, I had to hide it. Hence my toilet-roll alibi, sitting on the granite boulder next to me, a glowing orb in the moonlight. I wouldn't need to use one for days yet. Not after living on bush food and doing this much walking. But I'd need my dope. Even thinking about going without made my body ache.

~

The night before, we'd cooked the abalone whole — upside down on the fire. They spun in their shells and lapped at the air like cow's tongues until they died. The boys looked on like footy supporters in the front row at the MCG: not *in* the game, exactly, but close enough to feel like they had a stake in it. Jacob was the exception. He kneeled at the fire and poked the steaming shellfish with the glowing end of a stick until they were cooked. Said he'd done it all before — and probably had too. Hell, I knew my way around an abalone at his age. But I grew up over here. Some of the young fellas didn't eat much. Said they weren't hungry. It's always the same on these camps — for the first few days, anyway. Eventually their hunger overcomes the need for the familiarity of their usual diet.

We call these trips 'survival camps' because they are all about learning some of the old ways. Living off the land. To the old fellas, the tribal people — and even us mob who grew up on the islands — culture isn't something we try to learn or reclaim. It's what we are immersed in from the moment we are born. But these boys have been assimilated. *Townified*, we call it. Nothing to be embarrassed about. They may live in two worlds, but they are still mob. And they need to know what separates 'em from their Aussie mates.

Tonight, we crumbed the abs and cooked them in garlic butter. Anyone would have thought we'd laid on KFC or something — they went that quick. These camps weren't so hardcore that we couldn't have a few non-traditional items, like a frying pan or some condiments. It was a condition of the funding, and something old mate Chris had a hand in. Couldn't be *too* traditional. *Survival camp* sounds great on paper, but the survival of the kids can never really be at stake. Traditional food, yarns, roughing it — that was about as far as it went. They could bring a sleeping bag and one set of spare clothes, but no phones or electronic devices. Chris had a satellite phone that could get coverage anywhere in the world, apparently — another tick on his safety list. I had my trusty old Nokia, which I would bet my ballsack had better coverage than Chris's fancy model. One thing I *did* insist on was that we found our own water, along the way. Chris was a bit cagey about that, so he brought some water-purifying tablets. We all had water bottles and filled them at every clear creek we came to. I have all the watering places mapped out in my mind. I grew up here, after all. I know this coast like most people know their backyard. But there wasn't as much water as I'd anticipated this time. It had been a dry year.

~

'Come on, boys,' said Chris the next morning. He was at the fire, building it up. 'Sun's coming up. Uncle Ben's got more plans for us today.' The boys were all sleeping on the thin, grey tarpaulin we'd brought along, to keep them off the sand. It was so wrinkled and old it looked like elephant skin. I was the only one with a decent camping mattress, thin as it was. And I had one of those expensive waterproof sleeping bags. I insisted on it — another condition of my employment.

'Mornin,' Chris. Damn, bruz, that smells good.'

'What's the plan today, then?' he asked, a few minutes later, kneeling next to me and handing over a steaming cup. Survival camp or not, I wasn't going without my morning coffee.

'Gunna show the boys how to set a snare this arvo, when we set up camp,' I said. 'Hopefully we'll get us a roo. Apart from that, we'll walk up the coast and I'll get 'em back in the water at low tide. They can gather some limpets and warreners.'

'We're pretty much out of drinking water, just so you know. I think the boys have finished their bottles,' he answered.

I did know about the water situation. And I was aware it was my job to keep on top of it. But I hated Chris pointing it out like that. Had the boys been awake and listening, I would have dressed him down, right and proper. He was a 'plan man.' Organized. Always wanting to know what's next.

Well, that's not how our fellas work.

'There's a good creek, just around the point,' I said. I held my cup upside down, shook it a few times and looked over toward the coffee pot on the fire. He took the hint.

~

'Which one of you boys has got my tin?' I asked the group, as calmly as I could.

They were lined up. All their gear was packed and we were ready to move on. The sun was still low in the east, but we should have been on the move before now. I was holding everything up, looking for my dope. The plan had been to get up before the boys and do my morning 'business,' but my tin wasn't where I'd left it, in the pocket of my pack. It wasn't anywhere at all that I could see. I had even retraced my steps back to the last spot I'd had a chuff.

Not a fucking thing.

'What tin, Ben?' asked Chris, after the boys didn't respond.

'Just a yellow tin. I keep my medication in it. Come on, I know one of you boys has it. I won't be mad if you give it back now.'

'Righto, crew! Let's all pitch in and look around the camp for Uncle Ben's medication,' ordered Chris.

The boys had a half-arsed look around the camp, kicking at the sand and leaves. I went through my pack again. The tin definitely wasn't there. When I asked the boys to empty their packs too, they all did. Chris stood back, while I went through their gear.

'I know one of you has it. It was in my bag last night and now it's just magically disappeared?'

'There is no medication listed on your registration form, Ben,' said Chris, almost as a whisper. He was squinting down at his folder, flicking through the pages.

Jacob spoke up. 'Maybe one of your spirits took it. Kutikina, was it? The one you went on about last night, who you reckoned was gunna get us if we played up.'

I caught his smirk. *Smart-arse little fuck.*

I knew, then, that *he* was the one who had my tin.

'Righto, you mob. If that's the way it's going to be … Let's go, then.'

~

We kept the beach on our right side for about an hour and a half, until we reached a rocky headland, and then we veered left, away from the coast. The track followed a natural cobble formation that was difficult to walk on. The boys were doing it tough — as were my knees, although I didn't let it show. The track gradually disappeared and soon we were picking our way through thick poa-grass plains, using the flat granite outcrops as stepping stones. It wasn't exactly a straight line, but we were heading in the direction I wanted.

'Looks like we've left the path you mapped out,' announced Chris, after the boys had started falling behind. He stopped and turned in circles, using his body to shield his GPS screen from the sun's glare. 'Says here we're supposed to hug the coast until we get to Deep Cove.'

'I thought we could take a short cut, Chris. If that's okay with you? Means we won't be getting water for a while, though.'

'Didn't you say there was a watering place around the point back there?'

A slight whine had crept into Chris's voice, and I noted it with a smile as I powered on ahead. It would take me weeks to get my knees right, after this. But at least I wasn't as dehydrated as the rest of them — I had an extra water bottle and was sipping on it secretly when I was out of sight.

Chris was a fit-looking guy: one of those slim fellas who jogged regularly (in brand-name active wear, no doubt, and probably with a club or one of those wanky boot camps). Today, though, he was sweating for the boys. Their wellbeing was his responsibility, and nobody except me had had anything to drink since we'd left camp that morning.

The waterhole up ahead, I remembered, was an old tin-mining site. A Chinese exploration team had dug out a creek bed back in the 1800s. When I was a kid, the old fellas said it was haunted, that it had caved in on some of the workers and their bodies were never recovered. But the old fellas thought everything was haunted, so I didn't believe it for a minute. It was one of the stories I'd been planning on passing off as undoubtedly true, though, at that night's camp fire.

But between here and there was a large hill. And we were going to go over it.

After that, if things went to plan, we would head back to the coast. It was about two hours' walk from the waterhole. We would make camp there for the night and I'd smoke two joints to make up for the one I'd missed that morning. I hadn't been this straight for years and my mind was racing, like a crazy bastard.

~

'Ben, we're going to have to take a break,' said Chris, part way up the hill.

I looked back to where the boys had stopped walking. They had formed a circle around Rhys, the youngest, who was bent over, trying to breathe. By the time Chris and I reached them, he had started crying. In the presence of the adults — the responsible ones — his few breathless tears swelled to a racking sob. Jacob sat on a rock by himself, and stared defiantly out across the ocean.

'He … they … we all need water,' said Chris, sounding desperate.

'Listen up, you fellas,' I said.

They all looked at me, even Jacob. Rhys's chest was still heaving, but there were no more tears. They had dried up.

'I know where there is a waterhole, very close to here. A cold, fresh waterhole — big enough to swim in.'

'Great. Finally,' said Chris, with more than a hint of impatience. *The man has balls after all.*

'However,' I said, and then paused for dramatic effect, 'I'm only taking you there when the sly fucker who stole my tin returns it.'

~

The chopper swooped in about two hours after Chris's call. It landed on the top of the hill. I was the last to get in. I gave the boys one last chance to return my dope. But none of them would meet my eye. The only one who made eye contact was Chris, who wore a sorry frown. It was a look I'd seen before, which said, *It's out of my hands.*

Losing my stash was the only reason I was happy to leave the island. I'd miss this place. I'd miss this job — even though the kids were a pain in the arse, it felt good to be back here, passing on my knowledge. Leaving early wouldn't cost me anything, financially. My contract stated that I got paid in full, even if the trip was canceled or called off prematurely. Besides, Chris was the one who'd pulled the plug, and I'd be making damn sure that point was well known to everybody.

'It's for the safety of the boys,' he'd said.

They certainly didn't seem disappointed to be leaving. In fact, as the chopper rolled off the hill, following the southern ridge down toward the coast, they seemed pretty damned excited. I'd been in plenty of choppers and was used to the exhilaration. I guessed this was their first time. As the trees opened up, I craned my neck to see the waterhole at the old tin mine. I wanted to point it out to the boys — and to Chris, in particular. To show them what they had missed out on. But the light that caught my eye wasn't the familiar glint of silvery water. It was the glittery sparkle that comes from mica in river sand. There was no water.

Not a fucking drop.

I rested my head back on the seat and rubbed at my knees. I looked over at the city kids, in their brand-name clothes, happy to be going back to their creature comforts.

I peered back out the window, at the dried-up mine, becoming smaller and smaller as we flew away.

Jacob saw too. I know he did. His gaze had followed mine. The other boys gathered around Chris, who was passing out drinks from a cooler in the chopper. Grateful hands patted his back.

Jacob refused his drink. We just stared at each other knowingly.

It was me who looked away first, to study my weeping knuckle where I had tried to light the flint.

Perhaps this *would* be my last camp. Things had certainly changed since I lived on the island all those years ago.

There had always been water back then, there at the old tin mine. Always.

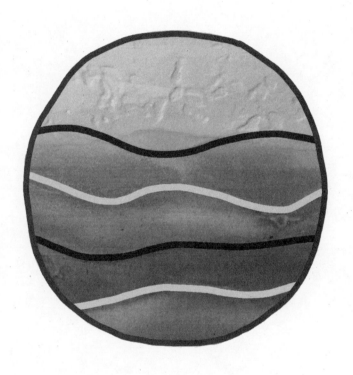

HONEY

'So, Nathan, what is the Aboriginal word for *honey*?' asked Sharkey, as he swung the ute into a sharp right-hand turn.

Nathan looked left out of his open window, into the steep ravine known as the Elephant Pass. A ghostly afternoon mist clung to the ferns and trees that lined the gorge. He could feel his hair dampening from the cool air coming through the window.

'Not sure,' he replied, absently.

'Well, you're Aboriginal, aren't ya? You should know,' said Sharkey.

'Yeah, well … I'm sure there is a word for *honey*, but—'

'Thought ya were going to find out for us. Wanna use the name on me label. Be a good gimmick for selling the honey, I reckon. 'Specially with the tourists.'

'Yeah, probably,' said Nathan. 'I'll look into it.'

'That'd be good. And cheers for giving us a hand moving the hives. Really need to get them on to the prickly box, now the kunzea has finished flowering.'

'Yeah, no worries.'

Nathan looked over at Sharkey and met his gaze. Sharkey liked to make eye contact when they talked in the car. Nathan thought it was a bad habit but obliged him anyway.

'Ya know what, Nath? I was serious when I said I'd give ya the ute if ya keep helping me out like this. I reckon you've just about earned it by now.'

'Cheers, man,' said Nathan.

They hit an intersection at the base of the pass, and Sharkey turned right onto the coast highway. The ocean appeared and disappeared as the undulating road wound its way through farms and forests. They pulled into a concealed driveway, overgrown with drooping she-oaks.

'Hives are just in there,' said Sharkey, pointing into the bush. 'Might want to suit up.'

Both men got out of the vehicle. Sharkey reached into a black fish bin on the tray and scruffed two wrinkled plastic bags. He threw one to Nathan. 'This should fit you.'

Nathan stared up at the sky. It was late afternoon and there was still plenty of light, but the sky over the ocean was darkening.

'Looks like rain,' he said, as he shook out his bee suit.

Sharkey was already zipping his up. He was one of those people who did everything flat out, making his fat, saggy face and body jiggle constantly. 'Yeah, well, that's why we need to get these hives blocked up. Fast.'

They climbed over the broken wire fence and made their way through the trees to the beehives, which stood out stark white against the green and brown hues of the coastal vegetation. Only two weeks earlier, the cottonwool-like kunzea flowers had been fragrant and alive with bees. Now, their dried and shriveled remains carpeted the ground, and the dank, piney smell of rotting she-oak needles layered the salty air.

Looking like spacemen in their white body suits and rubber gloves, the two men blocked up the hive openings with wads of crumpled catalogues, and heaved the bee boxes over the fence and onto the back of the ute. The disturbed cacophony coming from the boxes rose a few octaves as the bees were tossed about. The vibrations surged through Nathan's fingers like mild electricity, causing the muscles in his forearms to flutter. The bees that had been shut out of their hives smashed themselves into his mesh veil, trying to get to his face. Their menacing, high-pitched buzzing put him on edge.

'Man, there's some honey in these,' said Sharkey, as they shuffled the heavy hives around on the tray. 'I'll make some decent coin out of this.'

While Sharkey roped on the load, Nathan wandered down toward the sea and found a clearing surrounded by coastal wattles. He bent over and picked up a smooth stone that seemed out of place. It bore markings that he had seen before. Searching around the immediate area, he observed several more stones just like this one. He picked up another. It had a waxy sheen, and a long, serrated edge that appeared as if it was sharpened only days before. It fit snugly into the palm of his hand.

'What ya got there?' called Sharkey. He had already taken off his bee suit and was striding down toward Nathan.

'Stone tools,' replied Nathan, indicating with a nod to the scatter around their feet.

'Give it here,' said Sharkey. His pudgy hand shot out and snatched the stone from Nathan's grasp, and he held it up to the remaining sun as if to see through it.

'Trust you to find this,' said Sharkey, raising his eyebrows. He brought the stone close to his face, squinting at it while rolling it through his fingertips. 'Don't go tellin' the rest of yer mob what ya found here. Bloody … next thing ya know there'll be a land rights claim on me honey turf.'

'It doesn't work like that,' said Nathan, suppressing a sigh. 'We can't just claim land rights anywhere that we find artifacts.' He expected a cocky remark but one didn't come. 'Anyway, all along this coast is the same. You can see where the old people camped and lived.'

'Yeah, whatever,' said Sharkey. He flicked the stone tool off into the bush and paced back toward the car. 'Let's get the fuck-off outta here. Don't worry about taking off ya suit.'

Drops of rain peppered the windscreen as Sharkey backed the ute out of the driveway, its rusty leaf springs groaning as it labored over the potholes.

'There's some weight in her,' said Sharkey, smiling. He was in a better mood, now the hard work was almost done. All that was left was to put the hives at the new location. Sharkey got the ute up to highway speed, checking in the mirror to see how the hives were riding, then reached his hand behind Nathan's seat to extract a six-pack cooler.

'Drink?' He pulled a can of rum and Coke off the plastic ring and pointed it at Nathan.

'Got one, thanks.' Nathan took a Fanta from the cooler down by his feet, wiped the top of the can on the leg of his bee suit and opened it. It was cold and gassy, and burned the back of his parched throat. Sharkey expertly opened his drink with one hand and took a swig. He rested his rum on the seat between his legs, pulled a half-smoked cigarette from the ashtray and lit it. The ute swerved a little as he took his hands from the wheel.

'Those stone tools back there. They're not that special, ya know?' said Sharkey. He took several drags on his cigarette and, with the last one, blew a smoke ring at the windscreen.

'Well—' Nathan began.

'Growing up, me and me cousins spent all our time down at the river. We lived up at Smithton, and the river was just across the paddock from our house.' Sharkey wound down his window and flicked out the cigarette butt. In the side mirror, Nathan watched the butt explode into a shower of sparks on the slick road and spin off into the night. Sharkey shivered dramatically as the cold rain blew in, and quickly wound up the window.

'We used to skip stones a lot, and we would set shitloads of deadlines. We'd go back in the morning and check 'em before school. Always got fish — although many of 'em would be float-ing by the time we got to 'em. Anyway, Uncle Murray — Mum's brother — he used to come and stay with us sometimes. One day, we took him down the river and he found these stone tools — like those ones you found today, only there were heaps more of 'em.'

Sharkey finished his can and threw the empty into the back. He lit another cigarette, drew in deeply and exhaled as he continued.

'Uncle Murray said the blackfellas used the stones to cut things because they weren't smart enough to invent knives. He said that if Grandad and the other farmers ever found stone tools on their land they would bury 'em or throw 'em in the river so that your mob couldn't come along and claim land rights.'

Nathan could sense Sharkey smiling at him, but he refused to meet his gaze. He pulled off his beanie and ran his thumbs over the rough embroidery of the Aboriginal flag.

'Anyway,' said Sharkey, 'when me uncle left, we looked all along the river and found heaps more patches of the bloody things. Hundreds of 'em — all different types, ya know? Different colors and that.'

He slowed down the ute and turned left onto the Elephant Pass road. He glanced in the rear-view mirror again to check the hives as they began the steep ascent and rounded the first few sharp bends. Satisfied the hives were sitting well, he turned back to Nathan.

'Nath, do ya know what a duck-fart is?' he asked, breaking the silence.

'No,' Nathan said. A lie — he had some idea of what it was.

Sharkey cracked a fresh can and drank half in one go. He burped loudly and blew the gassy stench toward Nathan. 'It's when ya throw a stone up into the air and it lands in the river, making a funny sound. You have to get a thin sort of stone — rounded so that ya can wrap yer finger around it. When ya throw it up into the air, ya have to get a good backspin on it. If ya throw it right, when it lands in the water, it doesn't make a splash. It makes a kind of "plop" sound. That's why it's called a duck-fart.'

Nathan, quiet, stared down at the beanie in his lap. He knew where this was going.

'Those stone tools along the river — the ones yer ancestors knocked up — they made the best duck-farts. They are like the perfect type of rock for it.' Sharkey laughed to himself and looked over at Nathan expectantly.

'Me and me cousins would have thrown thousands of them into the river, in those days. I doubt there would be any left around there now. But ya can't get away with that anymore,' he said, chuckling. 'Can ya?'

'Nuh,' was all Nathan could muster. He noticed his hands were trembling.

'Hope I'm not offending ya,' said Sharkey smugly.

Nathan shrugged, and looked back out of the window.

Sharkey slurped up the last of his drink and dropped it on the floor. He turned the wipers up a notch to combat the now-pelting rain. 'These bloody cans are going down a bit too nicely,' he said. 'Let's hope the local cop isn't out and about tonight.'

For the next few kilometers neither of them spoke, and Nathan was grateful for the peace. As they got close to the top of the pass, Sharkey grabbed another cigarette from the dash console, and put it to his mouth. He fumbled with the lighter and it fell to the floor in front of him. Nathan watched him stretch down for it, his fingers probing the dirty, worn carpet below his seat. As he dropped his head below the wheel to take a look, the ute swerved again, and this time the tray clipped the steep, rocky wall of the pass. The back end slid out, fishtailing, and Sharkey tried to correct the vehicle by swinging heavily on the wheel. The ute lost traction on the wet road, flipped onto its roof and went skidding into the guardrail on the cliff side of the road. Even from his upside-down position, Nathan could see the rail buckle and wave as they struck.

For a moment, the only sound was a hissing from the tires or the engine and the scattering of window glass. Within seconds, though, a droning sound rose, and grew steadily louder. Nathan looked over at Sharkey, who was also hanging upside down. Sharkey's eyes were glazed over. His nose was broken and bent at an obscene angle, and his wavy, black hair was plastered across his wobbling face with blood and something else.

Honey.

The drone was turning into an angry roar. Nathan felt something dangling against the back of his neck. He reached around and felt for the hood of his bee suit and drew it over his head. His hands were shaking as he fumbled to pull the zips from the back around to the front, sealing it off.

He twisted his head to see the beehives lying scattered along the road, some piled up against the guardrail. The individual boxes had come apart and the frames were oozing their sticky amber contents onto the asphalt. The light from the headlamps dimmed as the dazed bees took flight. Their roar was deafening. Sharkey was crying. The way his lips were drawn back from his teeth as his white, panicking eyes took in the scene before him reminded Nathan of the pony his sister had when he was a kid.

'Oh God … what … shit, help me, Nathan. Ya gotta get me outta 'ere!' Sharkey screamed above the din of the bees.

Nathan released his own seatbelt and, holding on to it, eased himself down to the ute's velour ceiling. He kicked the shattered windscreen out with his foot. Bees flooded in.

'Hey, where — hey, where are ya going? You can't leave me.' Sharkey's voice had a strange calmness — a sure sign that he'd lost it.

Nathan turned back to look at him. Sharkey had given up trying to release his seatbelt and was frantically swatting at the bees attacking his face. Nathan began to crawl out of the ute and was shocked at the sight in front of him. The headlights were almost completely blacked out by the dense swarm of bees. Their frenzied movement created a breeze that Nathan could feel even through the mesh of his veil.

The crumpled ute pitched and squeaked as Sharkey thrashed in his seat. Nathan crawled through the wall of bees and out onto the road. He slip-slided his way through the honey and smashed-up wax until he reached the guardrail and pulled himself up. On his feet now and with the dim lights of the ute behind him, he stumbled up the road into the dark. As if on cue, the rain stopped. The noise of the bees grew quieter as he rounded the first bend.

With a steady hand, he unzipped the hood of his bee suit and let it slide from his head. His beanie dropped to the ground and he retrieved it, holding it to his chest. The air felt good and cool on his face. A car would come along soon.

As he walked up the dark road in a calm daze, a faint smile came to his lips. *What* is *the Aboriginal word for* honey?

BORN INTO THIS

The air was so crisp as Kara stepped out of the car that her first breath became a gasp and the inside of her nose burned. She leaned into the passenger seat of her beat-up red Corolla and reefed her puffer jacket out from under the mountain of clutter. The heat of the interior caressed her face like a warm hand and she almost succumbed to the temptation to get back inside.

Her jacket rustled and swished as she slid into its pillowy folds. The sound silenced a frog that had been noisily protesting the invasion of its puddle by her bald front tires. Kara closed her eyes and attempted to shut off her thoughts. She was still in work mode, having left the office — *thank fucking fuck* — only thirty-eight minutes earlier. Allowing her shoulders to relax, and her breathing to lengthen, she engaged in her own custom meditation. Her senses amplified. The sunlight, filtering through her eyelids, was a healing beam of energy projected at her by her tribal ancestors. The magic was broken by the ticking and clanking of the Corolla's cooling engine.

Time to get moving.

Kara started walking. At the beginning of the trail, a sign read: *Mount Barrow Reserve. Two hours return.* The high sun cast short shadows, reminding her that it was early afternoon. Today was her half-day Friday. Part way through last year, and after thirteen hard-slog years at the organization, she'd requested a four-day week but had been denied.

'If you can do your job in four days, why the hell have we been paying you for five?' her manager, Jason, had said. Kara tried to explain that she would have to drop some duties, but he waved her away. *Cockhead.* Kara had wanted to tell him where he could stick his job, but remembered the mounting bills on her kitchen bench and stayed silent.

Jason was a tick-a-box Aboriginal and could never prove his identity. But he had management credentials and waltzed straight into one of the top jobs. Suddenly an expert on everything black. The compromise had been a half-day off, once a fortnight. Unpaid, of course. Still, it was better than nothing, and Kara vowed to herself to make it worthwhile. Somehow.

The beginning of the track was easy and she walked briskly. The world gradually dropped away on her left as the track rounded the first incline, and she unzipped her jacket slightly and pulled her jumper away from her chest, fanning it. Stopping to catch her breath, she took in the view. Below her, the angular mountain scree tumbled down into a dark gully — and she took an involuntary step back from the edge.

The landscape was sparse, but far from boring. Mosses of brown, green and white clung to rocky overhangs and jagged branches, reminding her of her grandfather's wispy beard. Snow gums erupted from the shattered shale, their twisting boughs flexing skyward, like fingers on an upturned hand. From the lookout, Kara could see the track snaking along the side of the ridge.

About a hundred meters ahead, unnatural colors flashed through the trees. *People.* Kara paused for a moment and then slipped into the nearest thatch of scrub on the edge of the track, clipping her knee on a concealed boulder as she did so. She let out a muted scream: the kind a child wakes up with, following a nightmare. She crouched down, lost her balance and sat back into a half-frozen puddle.

Fucking idiot.

She made herself as small as possible, but then became pre-occupied with the pain in her knee and the numbing wetness spreading across her backside. She closed her eyes and tried to calm herself with more meditation — but the discomfort prevailed, and she gave up. Kara sat there, willing silence, but with every ragged breath, every cold shudder, fern tips and sheaths of dry bark scraped against the parachute material of her jacket.

As the crunches and scrapes of the walkers grew louder, Kara held her breath. She timed it badly, though, and just before they got to her she exhaled sharply, almost coughing in the process. The strangers passed, oblivious to her presence. A middle-aged couple, slim and fit. The man had an odd-shaped but well-clipped beard. The woman wore a designer hiking outfit in retro pastel colors. Kara could tell that they weren't from around here. They held themselves — as did all white mainlanders — with that peculiar, assured air. It made them seem taller and more upright than the locals. Kara hadn't seen their car — which must have been in the bottom car park — but she formed a mental picture of a bright-orange Subaru wagon, with ski racks and hexagon-patterned alloys.

Heaving herself up, she stumbled back onto the track. The couple's scent still lingered there, fresh and modern. She squeezed the damp seat of her jeans and felt water trail down the back of her left leg to her sock. Swinging a wild, angry kick at a pile of wombat droppings, she aggravated her knee even further. It was time to admit it: she was having a bad day. This walk was meant to turn it around but it was failing dismally.

~

Kara was the receptionist at the Aboriginal housing co-op in Launceston. She was the face, the voice, the first point of contact. She was used to copping shit, but that didn't make it any more palatable.

When the woman had barged in that morning with her son, and stood boldly in front of the counter with her hand on her hip, Kara knew what was up. She'd seen a thousand Johnny-come-latelys and had observed there were two main types: the ones who played the sympathy card, and the ones who tried to intimidate you into accepting them. This woman and her son were the latter kind.

'We want our Aboriginal papers, please. We just found out his father could be Indigenous.' The woman added 'please' through gritted teeth, and Kara wondered why she even bothered.

'Has your son ever used our services?' asked Kara, following protocol. She knew perfectly well that the boy had never stepped foot inside their doors.

'No, of course not. We only just found out.' The woman pushed her son toward the counter. 'Here, tell her,' she said to him.

With a pudgy hand, the boy pushed a tuft of fringe off his pocked forehead. 'Yeah, my aunty says we're Aboriginal,' he muttered. 'And that we can get stuff … you know, for free.'

Kara looked to the woman, waiting for her to scold the boy. As unscrupulous as the Johnny-come-latelys were, they were rarely so open about their intention to scam benefits. The woman just stared back at Kara, eyebrows raised in question.

Here we go again.

Her manager was lurking, and Kara knew — and resented — that he expected professionalism from her in the face of such crap.

'Our policy is—' began Kara, half smiling to herself in resignation.

'I don't care what your policy is,' interrupted the woman. She shifted her weight to the other hip and waved a finger at Kara's face. 'I want papers for my son, saying he's Indigenous. And don't you fucking smirk at me.'

Kara raised her hand, her instincts to fight kicking in.

I'll rip that finger off.

She felt a colleague's hand on her shoulder. 'No, my girl.'

~

Kara eased her legs back into motion, and pushed on. The trail clung to the ridge for about half a kilometer before it came to a junction. An arrow indicated that the main trail went left, but Kara looked to her right, where the trail was narrower and less worn. The bush there was different: dense manuka scrub dominated the undergrowth and loomed over the track, forming a low tunnel. She took it as more of a wallaby run than a human trail. She flipped her hood over her head and shouldered her way down the overgrown path. The smell of the vegetation, as it closed in around her, carried her back to her childhood, to a time when her great-grandmother washed her in an old kerosene tin that lived on her rear step. A capful of ti-tree oil in the scalding water, and she was scrubbed with a stiff brush and harsh lye soap until tears came.

'If we can wash this black off, might be hope for you yet,' her great-grandmother would say, on every occasion.

~

Kara came to an old forestry road at the end of the bush tunnel and continued back onto the main trail. Nature had reclaimed the road. It was lined with cat ferns, giving it a stately appearance and feel. This track, she thought, could lead to her very own secluded rainforest mansion. There'd be large bay windows. A steaming jacuzzi. All the stuff rich people had. And nestled in the corner of a sunlit reading room would be a neat desk — not one piled with clutter and bills. Somewhere to sit and do useful things — maybe write a book, or letters to the papers, sticking it to the racist white politicians — as she liked to do but rarely had time. The days would be pleasantly, almost wearyingly, long. And the nights would arrive like an unexpected yet much-welcomed visitor.

Such was her fantasy life — one far from her own. What she'd first thought would come with the nine-to-fiver was late in the mail, or lost, as she was now beginning to accept. Fair enough, she was earning an average wage, but she was worn down from still being in a continual state of debt, and by the envy she felt toward others who were doing it far easier than her.

Working poor, yeah right. White privilege more like it.

She winced at the thought — it felt like an excuse. Deep down, she knew she just wasn't good with her finances.

~

The road came to an open glade, and Kara sat down on a hairy tree stump. Her behind and legs were numb from cold. She longed for the warmth of the sun on her skin. Beneath her feet, sphagnum moss carpeted the ground.

Finally, rainforest country.

Man ferns adorned the edges of the glade, their foliage poised like giant jumping spiders. Kara surrendered to her favorite vice and lit her first cigarette since the car. She recalled when smoking was popular: the fabric of the office social sphere. Since her big boss had decided to quit, it had become increasingly frowned upon in her workplace. Now she was part of the office minority: pariahs, exiled to the alley next door for a few dirty minutes of every working day.

I'm free out here, she thought, watching the smoke form a thick, white cloud as it passed her lips and hit the chill mountain air. *Free, like the old people were.* Town life was inundating her in a flood of responsibility, repetition and despair that, more and more lately, she could feel lapping at her chin.

Kara jerked back to reality. She observed the shadows in the glade — how they had lengthened and now leaned toward her. The days were still short, although it was officially spring. The characteristics of this season resonated with Kara and she smiled inwardly at its arrival.

Time to get moving, again.

Just past the glade, the road fringed another decline. She'd walked across the top of the ridge and was on the other side now, and the view from here was completely different. Forestry had been active on this side, and reaching to the mountains in the distance was a patchwork of tree plantations, at various stages of growth. Here and there, random sections of vegetation had been cleared back to bald earth, making the landscape look like a huge, incomplete jigsaw puzzle.

The first time Kara stood at this spot, she'd melted into tears, and the noise of her emotions drifted across the valley. She was fragile, at the time, overwhelmed by life, relationships, money. The vision of the land — her ancestors' country, so far removed from the cultural landscape it once was — took her over the edge. She cried uncontrollably, unashamedly: the way you can when you're alone. It was in those reflective moments, with the clarity that followed this meltdown, that she resolved to put her plan into action.

Kara left the track again. She zigzagged her way downhill, using tufts of grass and dry logs to keep her balance. Toward the base of the hill, she crouched in the ferns and scanned the area below for activity. Where the slope met the flats, a caterpillar-like trail of thick manuka, interspersed with eucalypt crowns, hugged the contour. This was the creek: almost the only natural vegetation left in the valley. Forestry weren't allowed to touch the creek. It was protected, off limits. Kara loved that. She smiled to herself. It felt, to her, like a small win.

Continuing downhill, she hit the creek and followed it, listening to the tinkle and plunk of the water. She crossed the creek where a log had got jammed, with her arms out like a high-wire performer. She checked the log for footprints. Only hers, still there from the previous week. Entering the first coupe, she marveled — as she always did — at how the small pines looked like a field of Christmas trees. The soil was clumped and compacted underfoot. Kara could still make out the dozer tracks from when the land was cleared. As she walked between the rows, she studied the ground for the signs of her people.

Growing up, she had spent a lot of time on country: camps, day trips, events. Her uncle — now dead — worked as an Aboriginal heritage officer, before all the jobs were farmed out to white archaeologists. As a teenager, she would often spend days helping him and he would pay her, generously. It was a time she recalled fondly, a period of contentment when opportunities were boundless and time seemed insignificant, before the draining veil of responsibility had settled.

Back then her job was to look for stone tools. Her uncle said her eyes were much closer to the ground than his. When she found them, he would take photographs and mark them on a map. He had a unique way of bringing each tool to life. He would explain to Kara how they were formed, used, why they were left the way they were. He told the story of the people who made the tools, and how they moved through country. He showed her where they camped, explained how they hunted. Kara would close her eyes while he spoke and picture the old people going about their lives. When she opened them, she felt like she could still see them. In her mind, they were still there.

She continued now through the pines, pausing a few times to inspect stones. Eventually she came to a dip in the valley where the trees thickened. They reached her chest, some to her head, and she had to force her way through. She stopped once or twice, straining her ears for sounds. She pushed her way into a small clearing and found herself against a wall of chicken wire. It was painted black, and was barely visible. Kara ducked to the ground. Being here didn't put her in danger, but the forestry workers, if they found her, wouldn't take too kindly to her actions. She knew from her own research that what she was doing was against the law.

Yeah, the white law.

Hunkered down at the base of the fence, Kara waited: silent, listening. Then she stood and peered into the cage. The plants were in various stages of growth. Some a foot tall, others just fresh new seedlings. All were in black pots and spaced as efficiently as possible within the cage. The bright-green luminescence of young eucalypt leaves distinguished them from the surrounding monotony of introduced pines. She tried to recall how many she had raised and planted, but had lost count. All grown from seeds she had collected, from the few remaining natives — their will to survive unshaken by the destruction of their environment, their roots so well established as to sustain the mechanical and chemical onslaught of the forestry operations. These were the best stock for her to propagate.

Natural survivors, like her own family, born into a hostile world and expected to thrive. She took in the surrounding devastation and thought again about her own life.

Born into this.

Kara walked back into the rows to where she had finished her previous work here, and tore a few pines from the ground. With each of these trips, she could feel they were getting more established and harder to remove. She replaced them with some of the larger eucalypts from her cage, caressing their young, succulent roots with her bare hands as she removed them gently from their pots. She patted the soil in around them and stared at them for a while with proud affection. It was like looking into a mirror.

Eventually the pines here would be too large to replace, and she would have to move her nursery to another location and start over. Her actions were never going to make a real difference, or solve her money problems. She knew that. But she was out of the office and away from her desk. She was walking, still, with her uncle, fulfilling some cultural obligations in her own small, secret way. Rich people might have all the trimmings, but they couldn't buy this type of satisfaction.

Kara gathered the two large buckets that were leaning against the cage. They, too, were painted black. Taking one in each hand, she climbed out over the cage and made her way to the creek for water, the lowering sun finally warming her back.

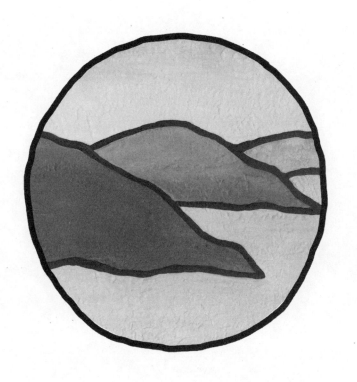

INVASION DAY

Stand out!' yelled stiff-legged Jack.

Through the amplifying harshness of the megaphone, he sounded like a dictator.

He turned to me. 'Stand out, brother,' he said, in the melodious yet graveled tones of his natural voice.

In his day, stiff-legged Jack was a national leader and a balls-to-the-wall activist. He was our hero, really. Even in retirement, he is on the news every couple of weeks — agitating, pushing our interests. People around noticed he had singled me out, and a hand patted my shoulder. I felt important.

A chant rose from the front and it spread like a Mexican wave. Missing the first word, I broke in on the next. I could hear my voice, clearer than those around me — making me self-conscious. I wondered if the other chanters experienced the same effect. A fat man with slick hair and a business shirt leaned against a traffic pole, shaking his head and clapping his hands slowly. He yelled at us to 'get a job.' Two police motorcycles barricaded the intersection and a string of cars waited. A horn bleated.

A half-full plastic water bottle swung in my hand. Lifting the bottom of my protest shirt, I eyed the padded bulge in my pocket.

And I shivered under the biting sun.

You're not going to chicken out, I told myself.

The *chink-chink* of clap-sticks gave rhythm to the chant. The hypnotic metallic ring echoed off the shop facades and the townhouses facing the street. I bounced along on the balls of my feet for a few steps, looking over the banners and bobbing heads for the dancers I knew. Streaked in elemental paint, they broke away from the front and, bent low to the footpath, wove their way back through the opportunistic spectators, with their phone cameras and takeaway coffees. One of the dancers, from my hometown, carried a spear and feigned a throw at an old Chinese couple, who clutched at each other and giggled, not wanting to lose face.

A short woman with a jowled face approached me from the side. I knew her through the community. She was from up the coast. I had been observing her as she started conversations with other marchers. She was uninterested in the protest, but she was there. She was a number.

'Did I tell you I've stopped drinking Coke?' she shouted into my ear and then waited for a response.

I gave her a thumbs up, then pointed at my ear and frowned. I hate chitchat during protests. It kills the mood. The chant heightened, and I took it up heartily, leaving the woman and her poor social skills to be swallowed up by the masses.

The lady in front of me must have been expecting cold weather: she was wrapped in a black puffer jacket and carried a small plastic Aboriginal flag on a wooden stick. I can always pick whitefellas at our events; they come with their banners and flags, but rarely hold them high enough to really stand out. A young girl ambling along beside the lady turned back to look at me and a bubble of watery snot burst from her nose and clung to her top lip. I bent down and straightened her oversized beret, which had slid down over one eye. She clung to her mother's leg, rubbing her face into her jeans.

'Spread out, people, and slow down.' The marshal ran alongside the footpath, bellowing and sweating into his loudspeaker. I slowed my pace. My throat was scratchy from yelling, and my lips felt desiccated. I should have brought another water bottle — one that I could actually drink from.

At the next set of lights, another police blockade waited with some media folk. A tall brunette reporter in a navy sports coat and fitted slacks scanned the marchers with an intensity akin to a cat monitoring its prey. She looked at me and then away. *Shame*, I thought. *She was cute.*

Then, after the intersection, a hand grasped my elbow lightly — it was the journo. Her dark fingernails rasped against my skin, giving me a tingle that followed my nerves all the way to my armpit. She looked over the top of her sunglasses at me, and her lips parted. I felt seduced, even though I knew she was just doing her job.

'Would you mind saying a few words about the march? About what Australia Day means to Aborigines?' she said, letting go of me. 'I'm with the *Tasmanian Herald*.' She took a notepad from her coat pocket and flipped it open.

'Sure,' I said. I relayed my opinions as she took notes. I babbled in my nervousness. When the loudspeaker came near, she leaned in close and I spoke into her ear. Strands of her hair blew into my mouth, and I tasted raspberries. She moved on, then, to the mother with the snotty pants. I felt a twinge of jealousy, but it faded fast as I remembered what I was planning to do.

'Go home, ya fucken wankers!'

Two teen boys and a girl with heavy make-up sat on the steps outside Franklin Square. The one who had called out had a skateboard resting across his knees.

'You go home, fuckwit. Back to Gagebrook,' said stiff-legged Jack, referring to the rough suburb on the far side of the river. He was by my side again, and we were cutting through the square, on our way to Parliament House. The teen's rant trailed off behind us.

Stiff-legged Jack hobbled forward at a surprising pace, unperturbed by the young hecklers. He raised the megaphone. 'Come on, you fellas. The fat cats'll be able to hear us from here. Let 'em know what we think of Australia Day.'

The crowd booed. Someone yelled out, 'Shame.' The footpath became a bottleneck as the police blocked us from walking on the highway. Up ahead, the dancers and the kids holding the large *Invasion Day* banner started crossing, moving down toward Parliament House Lawns. The march had stretched out to almost a kilometer, and I was somewhere in the middle. The chanting had ceased as we walked across the highway, but as the lawns and the gathering crowd came into view, the loudspeakers sparked up again, and the progressing throng found their second wind.

I experienced a twisting wrench in my stomach, a tightening chest. I took a deep breath but struggled to get air. It reminded me of a time I was given dope cake at a house party during college; I couldn't feel the air going into my lungs and panicked, thinking I couldn't breathe. My cousin Jimmy put me on the trampoline outside and talked me down until everyone else had gone home.

I felt for the package in my jeans. It was there. Part of me had hoped I'd lost it somewhere, so I wouldn't have to go through with it. *You'll be fine*, I heard Jimmy's voice say in my head. *No one's ever died from dope cake, and no one's ever died from what you're going to do.*

The protesters filtered through the stone gates onto the lawns. I was surprised at how succulent the grass looked. Looming above, like a love sonnet to colonialism, stood the sandstone monstrosity of Parliament House. To us, it was the physical man-ifestation of Australia Day, an ongoing reminder — a memo-rial, really — of the European invasion and all we had lost. A middle-aged hippy with grey pigtails and patchwork overalls gave it the finger as she passed through the gates, cursing the rotten bastards inside.

People gathered below the steps. Above them was an open area, bordered by a square, yellow hedge. This was our stage. A sound crew in black t-shirts fiddled with the PA as a group of official-looking people milled around. Stiff-legged Jack and others I knew were amongst them. Their faces became solemn as they readied themselves to take turns addressing the ravenous media, gathered there in numbers.

A dark man with a long grey beard tested the microphone and introduced himself as the MC. He wore one of the protest shirts, distributed to the crowd by the marshals earlier in the day. In bold, white capitals, it read: *CHANGE THE DATE*. The rally kicked off with a minute's silence, for the fallen heroes of the black resistance, and all the blackfellas who had passed on since. The crowd parted for a faux funeral procession, led by two wailing women Elders, arm in arm. Following the women were four community members, hauling a fake coffin constructed of thin plywood, painted matte black and adorned with eucalyptus branches and bright wattle flowers.

I felt a stab of envy toward the pallbearers. It was an honor to carry the coffin, something reserved for those who have fought in the struggle. I was overlooked, year after year, which was fine — I was young. But one of the pallbearers this year was new in the community. How had they got to be there? If I hadn't respected the ceremony, I might have sworn at them, out loud. Declared them a greenhorn in front of everyone.

To finish the ceremony, the dancers took up the branches from the lowered coffin and swept them across the ground in graceful arcs. They circled the funeral procession, stamping their feet in jagged motions and gripping the backs of their wallaby-skin cloaks with their spare hands.

The speakers then took their turns, each of them introduced by the enthusiastic MC. The first speaker was a shadow minister in the state opposition, who droned on about the failings of the current government and, in particular, their unwillingness to change the date of their Australia Day celebrations. The crowd cheered, and someone yelled, 'Shame.'

Short memory, people, I thought to myself, clapping along with the rest of them. This woman headed the previous government. While in office, she too had refused to change the date.

The rest of the speakers blended into one, with the exception of stiff-legged Jack, who spoke last. He described the atrocities committed against our people, in the days of the Black War. He recounted massacres that occurred around our island. His attention to detail was fascinating and gory, but he spoke an undeniable truth that made even the yobbos and the rednecks at the fringes of the crowd stare at the ground.

He ended on a positive note: 'There is, indeed, hope for the future,' he said, and indicated, with a hand gesture, to the large crowd.

I thought about what stiff-legged Jack said to me earlier. *Stand out, brother.* I knew what he meant. I knew what I had to do. Sometimes, it's your turn to stand out. And to stand up. Sometimes, it's just your turn.

Like I knew he would, stiff-legged Jack opened the mic up to the crowd. I was already making my way to the stage as he said the words. He nodded, as he handed over the microphone. I turned from him to face the people. *My people.*

'This is what I think of Australia Day,' I said. My voice sounded tinny through the PA, but it was clear and loud. I was heard. I pulled the bunched-up flag from my pocket and shook it out with one hand. I squirted the contents of my water bottle on it and held it high for the crowd. Spirits burned my eyes. The only sound was the whir of the cameras — as they zoomed, and panned, and closed in around me — and my heart, pulsing in my ears.

Holding my lighter against the dripping rag of red, white and blue, I thought of the fat businessman who'd told us to get a job, and the car that honked at the lights. I thought of the angry bogans, and the police who looked at us as though we were ants and they were the boots of destiny. But most of all I thought of the old people. *My old people.*

I thumbed the flint.

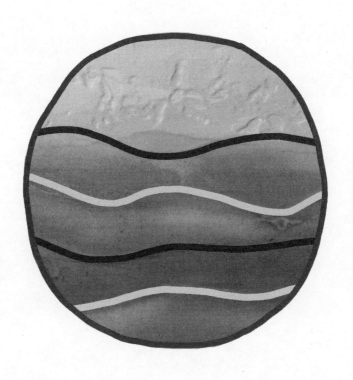

JACK'S ISLAND

The police boat moves toward Badger Island. It enters the small bay watched over by Jack's hut. His is the only hut on this side of the island, and the only one inhabited. Its occupation is betrayed by streaks of chimney smoke that stain the retreating sea fog above it. The hut is nestled amongst thick, green coast wattle above a small granite cliff. It is comfortable in its isolation, just like its owner. Both are unaccustomed to being disturbed.

The sound of approaching engines invades Jack's dream and he wakes, unsettled. The police boat circles around his bay, arrogantly declaring its presence. It is large, white and luxurious, with tinted windows and gaudy blue lettering on its side. It looks foreign amid its surroundings of ancient lithic structures, protruding from the mirrored sea. Or perhaps it is the islands — Jack's island in particular — that are out of place: trapped in another era and detached from the modern world.

Naked and bleary-eyed, Jack creeps to the window and peers over the sill. He watches the boat power its way across to the jetty. The party in blue take their time to disembark and hop across the boulders before disappearing into the tunnel of overhanging ti-tree leading away from the point. Once, the mere sight of police uniforms would have seized Jack's insides. Now, after years in isolation — years of reflection on the life he abandoned — he is impervious to their aura of fear and the threat of their authority. They are as redundant in his world as he is in theirs.

Jack takes his time to dress before leaving the hut. He observes the visitors soundlessly from his hiding place within a thatch of dense boobialla. There are five of them: three men and two women. The men stay at the edge of Jack's vision like ghosts. His eyes seek out the women, whom he studies with primal fascination. He sniffs desperately at the air for new scents. After years on the island, Jack has been cleansed of the pollutants that dulled his senses for much of his earlier life. He has become finely tuned to his environment. He has developed the ability to differentiate between native and foreign smells and can isolate and concentrate them in his mind.

As the police approach his hut, Jack catches whiffs of orange peel, crusty bread, washing powder, deodorant, lanolin and engine fumes. As if in response to some inner desire, a spiral of wind delivers to him a fleeting waft of femaleness: warm and perfumed and laced with the promise of contentment. With an impulsive shudder, Jack imprints this essence into his mind, to savor for as long as possible. Such small and once-insignificant things he no longer takes for granted.

Jack watches them leave. A white envelope on his rustic table, scattered footprints on the dusty track and an ephemeral trail in the ocean is all they leave behind.

Jack's eyes pass over the letter. He closes them. And he remembers.

~

The police courtesy visits happened a few times a year, when the large boat from Hobart took its tour around the Bass Strait islands. When they first started visiting, Jack would entertain them, making tea that they would sip, gingerly, from his stained and chipped cups. He would offer them a leg of cold muttonbird or a sugared doughboy, which they always politely declined. After Jack's Uncle Donnie left the island, he began to hide from unexpected visitors. He did not fear them — far from it. He was simply setting boundaries: any interaction with outsiders was on his terms, and generally only through necessity.

He'd first come to the island in 1997, on a trip organized by a local Aboriginal organization. Back then they'd brought large mobs of the community across to the islands to camp and explore. It was a way of returning to their roots — to the places where many of their modern families were established.

Of all the islands they visited, Jack felt the most at home on Badger. He was fascinated to learn about his own family's connection to the place. Above the grassy foreshore on the eastern side of the island, the camp leaders pointed out the ruins of old structures. One place, Jack discovered, had belonged to his great-grandfather, William Beeton. The remains of that hut consisted of a barely discernible granite foundation; strewn chimney bricks, darkened with soot and lichen; and a few scattered timbers. Some remnant garden vegetation survived: an agave plant, patches of naked ladies, and eggs and bacon daffodils — their appearance garish and exotic against the dullness of the dried summer grasses and native reeds. The hut faced the distant blue hills of Cape Barren Island — William's birthplace. To the west, and a stone's throw from Badger, was Chappell Island with the sinister volcano-shaped mountain at its center. Generations of the Beeton family ran muttonbird sheds there.

Jack left the island after the trip that day knowing he would return. But it was not the serene beauty or the call of his family's history that eventually brought him back. It was a prolonged bout of depression following the death of his infant son. In the darkness of those days, the solitude that came with the island's remoteness and isolation seemed like a slender ray of light. And for a long time, it was the desolate and lonely characteristics of the island that resonated deeply with the broken man.

Occasionally, planes would land on the airstrip, mainly because the absentee sheep farmer flew across from Flinders Island a few times during the year, most frequently during the shearing season. Jack came to recognize the unique drone and regular misfire of the farmer's plane and was familiar with all the planes that flew amongst the islands, and their schedules. Then one day, five years after he'd moved to the island, Jack identified the engine sound of one of the Cessnas belonging to a Launceston-based charter company. Their chief business was giving overpriced flying lessons to privileged kids. His curiosity sparked, Jack made his way to the airstrip to see his Uncle Donnie walk over the rise, shouldering a khaki duffel bag. His hair had thinned and his features had become more drawn since their last meeting, but he was still fit for his age.

None of Jack's other family had bothered visiting him, although they all knew where he was. The pretext for Donnie's visit was time out from work and travel. Donnie was Jack's great-uncle — his grandmother's much younger brother. He'd joined the army as a teen and married soon after. Strained from the extended periods Donnie spent abroad and remaining childless, the relationship failed. Donnie spent the rest of his working life traveling South-East Asia in gas and oil jobs. The envy of many, his lifestyle was a continuous cycle of rough and opulent: oil platforms to plush hotels; hard cabin bunks to the soft and inviting beds of the local women.

When Donnie's stay on the island extended beyond a month, Jack became curious about his uncle's intentions — and the real reason for his visit. He was very fond of Donnie; had anyone else just shown up like that, Jack would have run them off the island. But as time progressed, Jack began to appreciate the company. The despair that had driven him to Badger Island began to wane.

The two men spent their days improving the hut and tending to Jack's garden. Donnie was a keen fisherman and many a shadowy evening Jack would watch him from his garden on the cliff's edge, fishing rod and bucket in hand, crossing the chain of mottled granite boulders that linked to a larger rocky outcrop in the corner of their sapphire cove. There, Donnie had discovered he could catch silver trevally, when the wind was barely a breath on a swollen tide. The two of them lived mostly on what they caught from the sea and could grow in Jack's garden. Jack had become proficient with a throwing stick and, like his tribal forebears, would take an unlucky wallaby for protein when the relentless westerly winds made fishing impossible.

In autumn, when the earthy, seasonal smell of the mutton-bird colony drifted across from Chappell Island, they fashioned a crude raft from old fence posts and rusty oil drums. They paddled it across the seven hundred meters of rolling channel that separated the two islands, to harvest their *yula*, their muttonbirds. In the rocks of a sheltered gulch, they set a metal drum, which Donnie filled with seawater upon arrival. He lit a fire under the drum and fed it with scraps of salt-bleached driftwood he found jammed into rocky crevices and tangled amongst the seaweed at the high-water mark. High on his shoulders, Jack carried spear-loads of plump, downy muttonbird chicks in from the waving poa-fields. Together, they squeezed the amber oil from the chicks' stomachs and threw fistfuls of grey feathers into the wind, while the waves sucked the sand from under their feet and the mollyhawks danced in expectation.

After the plucking, Jack would go back in the rookery and leave Donnie to dunk the birds into the scalding pot and rub them back to a soft, white skin. Just like his grandfather had shown him, on this same island, when he was a boy.

With their quarry stashed in hessian bags, the two-man crew drift-paddled home to Badger on the retreating tide. There, they laid out their catch on makeshift racks of manuka branches to cool. In the evening, they removed the birds' extremities and insides before rubbing them in salt and packing their flattened pale bodies into casks. Salted and brined, the muttonbirds would keep for a whole year. When the desire arose — and it regularly did — they seasoned a few of their birds with Jack's dried herbs and ground native peppercorns. They cooked them on carved wooden skewers around beds of glowing coals. Rendered fat dripped from scores in the birds' crisping skin onto the fire, creating a pleasant grey smoke and adding another layer of flavor to the already delicious meat.

On such occasions, memories were aroused by the taste of their culture, and Donnie would recount stories of his childhood and Jack would listen intently.

The older man told of visiting Badger Island as a young boy. His grandfather William would sail them across from Launceston in a wooden cutter named *The Bella*. It was a long, wet journey in the unpowered boat, heavily burdened by people and supplies. Accompanying Donnie was his mother and three older sisters. They all stayed with William in his tiny hut, a rough and basic wooden structure with a skillion roof and only two small rooms. Surrounding the house was a ti-tree fence and a tended garden, full of bulbs and succulents. They all slept in one bed, except for William, who had a neat crib next to the fire.

Donnie never witnessed the old man sleep. Of a night, when he should have been slumbering himself, he would observe his grandfather quietly from his bed, through the opening between the two rooms. William would lean back in his handmade rocking chair in front of the dying fire, sipping cups of leaf tea and quietly humming to himself. Occasionally, he would reach into the fireplace and take a stick, which he used to light his pipe. As the tobacco flared, Donnie would catch the old man's face in the light. Fascinated by his brown, wrinkled forehead, long hooked nose and proud moustache, Donnie would wonder at the origins of this mysterious figure. As the flame died, William would blend back into the darkness where, as a dark, dark man, he seemed to Donnie to belong.

As Donnie's time on the island with Jack approached a year, Jack began to notice his uncle's failing health. The decline had been slow and gradual but now was very evident, although Donnie was quick to dismiss the matter when it was raised. His one remaining interest was their family's connection to the island. As time went on, this interest turned to fascination and then to obsession. Jack would accompany Donnie on his expeditions around the island in search of ruins and remnants of the old families' lives. They filled Jack's hut with all types of bottles and coins and buttons — treasures that they found or dug up. Donnie discovered a stash of broken inkwells, smothered by a century of discarded pine needles, under the great macrocarpa down by the jetty. He was adamant they once belonged to Lucy Beeton's school, the first school on the islands for Aboriginal kids.

One unnaturally still afternoon, under a violet, electrified sky and at Donnie's unrelenting insistence, they searched carefully through the pieces of a stone wall behind the island's old homestead. At the southern end of the wall, under a piece of glittering basalt, Donnie found a battered jam tin. The tin was so old that the hinges had seized and its lid had fused shut. Donnie's excitement over the find was contagious and the two practically ran back to Jack's hut with their find. Lingering thoughts of mortality brought on by Donnie's fading vigor were forgotten as they held counsel over the opening of the tin. After failed attempts using heat and muttonbird oil as lubricant, they finally cut it open with a rusty can opener.

Inside, bundled in a greasy cloth, was a large handful of gold sovereigns. They were English coins, with dates ranging between 1819 and 1823. The find was worth a fortune — they both knew it. But neither man, for reasons of his own, sought riches for himself. The true value in the find was in the history and the corroboration of their family's origins. Donnie reckoned that the coins belonged to the original Beeton, the whitefella who came out from London on a tall ship and discovered a relative peace on the islands, with an Aboriginal wife and family. Donnie was truly like a boy who had found where X marks the spot. His body allowed him this triumph and celebrated with a sudden return to health, for a few days anyway.

Then, just as unexpectedly as he arrived, Donnie left.

When Donnie didn't return one evening, Jack assumed that he had run out of daylight during his now-daily search expedition. But when the next silent evening came, he knew that Donnie was gone. No planes had landed, so Jack reasoned he must have departed, opportunistically, on a passing boat.

His uncle had left behind his bag and his treasures. The only item Jack found to be missing was his best length of rope — his strongest rope, the one they had used to lash their raft. Donnie even left behind his beloved gold sovereigns, which had already dulled considerably since they first opened the tin.

~

Jack picks up the envelope left by the police. His eyes flick past the writing on the front, careful not to read it.

What's the point of reading it?

It is a letter from Uncle Donnie, of course, with tales of his latest jaunts through Thailand and Vietnam, or musings over his past and his thoughts on being Aboriginal. How he misses his gold coins and, although he wishes he had taken them with him (to show off to his latest lady friend or his mates on the oil rig), he is glad they are still on the island, where they belong. That's all that will be in the letter. Why should he read it? He's got far too much to do.

Jack throws the envelope on the fire and walks outside. It is a hot day. He gets on his knees and works in the garden. After a time, he rises and wipes the sweat from his face with the inside of his t-shirt. He stands to full height, with his shirt raised to his chest, allowing the sea breeze to cool his body. His gaze moves across the horizon and over the islands in the distance. He can't believe the police were on his island, only hours earlier. Did that really happen? If it wasn't for the letter, now ashes in the fire, it might all have been a dream.

Jack's gaze lands on his island and sweeps across the dry landscape, past the agave plant on the foreshore and the ruins of William Beeton's hut, and settles on the dark she-oak forest nearby, where his eyes linger a little longer than he usually lets them.

SUMMER GIRL

You stare at me while I steer the old Holden through the bends. It's a look that says you will do anything for me — and I know you will. You have proven yourself on sweaty nights and lazy mornings. But not with love, so much as devotion.

'Where are we going to camp?' you ask, indicating the choice is mine. 'I can't wait until we're in the tent together.' You pull your legs up under you, allowing your whole body to face me.

My lower back hurts from the long drive and I stretch forward closer to the wheel and shift my hips from side to side.

'It's okay, baby,' you say. 'I'll massage you tonight.' Your husky tone envelops my brain and trickles down my spine like warm oil.

'Thanks,' is all I can manage, under the spell of you. It's a lame response but you don't seem to mind.

You spin the dial on the radio. Your fingernails are the color of ripe eggplant. As each station comes and goes, you watch my face intently. A mishmash of songs assembles out of the ether and dissolves again into the harsh hiss and crackle of static. The drone of a newsreader fades in and out, and something on my face — the slight deepening of the cleft between my eyebrows, perhaps — makes you return to the news channel.

'Cheers,' I say. And it is such a thin word, so out of place, when spoken to you.

You smile. The sun behind you, as we reach top of the pass, silhouettes your face and lights up the ends of your stray hairs, like fibers in an optic lamp.

We listen to the announcer give an update on some lost fishermen off the east coast, close to where we are heading. A local gardener comes on and gives autumn planting advice in an accent of red leather and aftershave. Michael Mansell is the next guest speaker. He explains how an Aboriginal treaty in Tasmania could work. He's really selling it. He makes it all seems so possible, so right.

You trace the barbed-wire tattoo on my wrist with your fingernail. Goosebumps spread to my upper arm, where a full-colored flag has been deeply etched.

'I support a treaty,' you say.

And, oh, do I believe you.

~

We stop for coffee at a general store. It's one of those country shops — the ones where the family lives out back. A teenage girl, with greasy hair and unbranded clothes, appears from behind an internal door to serve us. I catch a glimpse inside before the door springs shut. Cloth nappies hang on a wire rack before a wood heater — and somewhere further back, a loud American soap is drowning out a whingeing toddler. You order me a long black decaf, delivering the words with confidence. The upturned corners of your mouth betray your pride in remembering how I like it. On the counter, you place two large bottles of water. You tap the top of one with a hard fingernail.

'This one's for next to the bed,' you say with a wink before sauntering out with the goods, leaving me to pay. A bell is strung to the door with rough jute twine. Its jingle, so welcoming upon our entrance, sounds flat and false as the door shuts hard behind you.

~

'Tell me something,' you say, when we're back on the road. You are tucked up on the seat again, facing me.

'Like what?'

'I don't know. You're the writer — weave some magic.'

'Sorry, the gold is for the page,' I say, winking.

You think I'm joking, but the silent seconds that follow tell you I'm not. You pout and twirl your ponytail around your index finger. Turning back to the front, you find a music station with a song you like. It is 'Bad Medicine' by Bon Jovi, and you belt out the words into an invisible microphone. You shake off your sulk, jilting your body to the power ballad like a rock queen. It's well before your time and I admire, as I have before, your ability to transcend age.

The mood now lightened, I sing along with you. Your thin tie-dyed skirt has ridden up your legs and is bunching around your hips. You catch me looking at you and take my hand from the wheel and place it on your upper thigh. I hover my palm across the delicate peach fuzz on your bronze, unshaven skin. Your radiant heat is concentrated life: so pure. Everything else is death in comparison.

'Let's stop for a while,' you breathe into my ear.

I don't reply, but flick on the indicator and crane my neck for the next private place to pull over.

~

'Any spot you pick will be perfect,' you say, when we finally reach the coast. You sense my agitation and rub my back as we crawl along the dirt track.

Most of the camp sites are taken — full of families and college kids on their P plates. Dusty mountain bikes (shiny Christmas gifts only days earlier) lie on their sides on the edge of the road. Salt-crusted kayaks lean against the boughs of trees. Wet towels drape over the open doors of expensive 4WDs.

'Look at this, will you?' I say, as we pass a large camp, taking up multiple sites. They have created a compound using a shade-cloth wall. 'I bet one of them came and stuck a couple of little tents up here a few weeks before Christmas to secure this spot. It shouldn't be allowed.'

You are quiet while we look for a camp site. At the end of the track, you point out a small graveled alcove, hemmed in by drooping trees. It is not the pick of the camp sites, but it *is* empty — and now it is ours. I pull up the Holden and a dust cloud overtakes us. In the mirror, I notice that your cheeks are wet and your eyelashes have clumped together.

'I'm so sorry,' you blurt out, before I can react. You take my hand in between yours, rubbing it softly but vigorously, as if time is suddenly limited.

'For what?' I ask, cupping your face and swiping at your tears with my thumb.

'For what my people did to yours.' Your eyes well up again. 'You owned all the land and now you have to struggle — like now, just to get a camp at the beach.' Breaking into a sob, you collapse into me. The fullness of your chest heaves against my shoulder and your fingers dig at my arms in a kind of desperation.

If you could see my eyes right now, it would kill you to witness them roll in irritation. I suppress an annoyed sigh and calmly wait for you to settle. Your breath forms droplets on the skin of my neck and combines with your tears to pool in the hollow of my clavicle. Wanting this over, I bring our foreheads together, creating a space in which nothing but us exists.

'It's not your fault,' I say.

'You're so kind,' you whisper.

~

You walk barefoot around the camp, unconcerned about the bull ants and the broken glass. You are so much braver than me. We erect the tent together, but you refuse to let me help you make the bed. That's your nest to create — and I'm fine with that.

Teenage boys have taken to riding their bikes right up to our end of the road. They make a show of skidding their tires and doing tricks in front of our camp. You are good to them, waving and smiling each time they appear. The boys are all whispers and long stares. I admire the way you see the world, without malice and suspicion. You are so vulnerable that part of me wants to shield you, cup you like a butterfly, giving you just enough space to stretch your wings. Another part of me wants to squash you in my fist for being so naive as to land upon my open hand.

'Could you at least write me a poem?' you ask, returning to our conversation from the car.

'Sure.'

'What will you call it?'

'How about, "My Summer White Girl"?'

Your face lights up for a moment and then stiffens out, as you search for the meaning within the title. 'I would prefer just, "My Girl."'

~

After dinner you run ahead of me on the beach, laughing and doing cartwheels on the hard sand. Your skirt rides up your body, exposing your underwear for brief moments in the remaining sunlight. Campers spread out along the beach, twist their necks to see you: a brief distraction from their seaside comforts. Brand new reclining chairs with cup-holders. Iceboxes full of beer and juice boxes for the kids. Catch-buckets plastered with brand-name stickers, mostly empty. Some have tall surf-fishing rods, their lines reaching far out beyond the narrow channel where the smaller rods are cast, hoping their superior position will bring in the Big One.

You move to the water's edge, allowing the tide to flow around you. You summon me and I hug you from behind. A warm gust deflects off the sand, making your clothes and your hair swirl wildly. You push back against me. Your flesh is firm and molds to my body. Directly across from us, a long rock wall is breaking the rollers, creating a haven for boats to access the sea.

'Where is the Aboriginal heritage around here?' you ask.

I look upriver, following the edge of the bay as far up as the township of St Helens. Past the camping reserve, it is all private land, with houses and boatsheds built to the shore. Here and there, roughly sawn timber jetties, mottled with pale-green lichen, jut out into the water. The contour of the land has been shaped and manicured. I want to tell you the truth. I want you to know how my heritage along this coast has been bulldozed, smoothed over like warm butter on a crusty scone. The land formed into a fresh, new surface for the wealthy and the privileged to shape as they saw fit. You deserve to know the truth, but you are like a child in some ways. You look at me as a child does a parent, silently begging me to preserve your belief in the good of the world.

And your contentment is more important to me right now than the truth.

'Let's see if we can find something tomorrow. There should be some middens up the coast.'

~

Well after dark come the torches. You spot them first, rounding the bend before our beach. As they reach the front of our camp you call out. One of the search party approaches our fire. It's a police officer in an orange jumpsuit. He is handsome and young, but tired looking. His eyebrows are caked with day-old sunscreen.

'We're looking for the missing fishermen,' he says to you, ignoring me. 'We think they may have washed up along this part of the coast, possibly alive. We could do with some help in the search.'

Even in the dying firelight, you brighten up — invigorated somehow, by the thought of being useful.

'Can I?' you ask.

'I'll watch camp,' I reply.

You take the torch without another word and follow the policeman to catch up with the group, now some way up the beach. I listen until the calls of the search party meld into the roar of the waves on the ocean side of the point.

~

It is late when you return. You enter the tent quietly and undress in the dark. I have been waiting for you. My body, now accustomed to the makeshift bed, is hot and relaxed. You throw the covers over you and curl into a naked ball without a word. The wind picks up, shifting the trees. There is a light zipping sound as she-oak needles snap off their branchlets and slide down the tent. You recoil when I touch you, your skin like ice.

'I'm so cold,' you say. 'I'm sorry. I just need to sleep.'

'Did you find anything?'

'One of them ... washed up in the rocks ... what was left, anyway.' You shiver and I know it's not just the cold.

I should let you sleep but I need you right now. My mind keeps returning to your words in the car.

'Funny, isn't it? How the whole world turns out for a couple of white fishermen ...'

I let that sit in the blackness of the tent like a malicious entity.

'... when it was around here that the sealers abducted our tribal women and took them to the islands to be their slaves. And nobody came to *their* rescue.'

You roll over and press your nose to mine. I can smell the brine of your tears.

'Shhh, don't talk,' I say.

You spread yourself across me, engulfing me completely. You are my summer white girl — my delicate joey, hand-reared. I know that you will always return. You are devoted to me, indebted.

One day I will set you free, but not yet.

After all, summer isn't over.

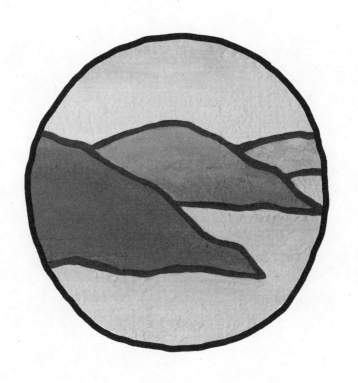

DESCENDANT

Ms McGregor cast her eyes around the room. 'How many students in this class identify as Aboriginal and/or Torres Strait Islander?'

Dorothy snapped a freckled hand toward the ceiling, oblivious to the ugly sweat mark at her armpit. 'I am.' She waited, uncaring, for the sniggers to come from the back of the class. And come they did.

The teacher looked straight through Dorothy and surveyed the rest of her Grade Ten social science class. 'Anyone else?' she asked with a sigh.

Dorothy waved her arm and wriggled in her chair. She was, after all, the chairperson of the ASPA committee. ASPA stood for Aboriginal Students and Parents Association. She'd convinced the principal to allow her to set up the ASPA committee three years ago, when she was in Grade Seven. She wrote to the Department of Education twice a week for almost an entire year until they eventually agreed to provide the funds.

~

Dorothy was a proud blackfella from a well-known family. Within her community, she was a *somebody*. She attended all the community events that she could make it to and had done so for as long as she could remember. Two years ago, she'd been picked to attend the Aboriginal Students Congress in Canberra, as the Tassie representative. The rest of the congress selected her to make a media announcement following their sitting. The whole thing made the national news and Dorothy enjoyed small-town celebrity status for the best part of a month. The following year, she won 'Aboriginal student of the year,' an award given out by her local Aboriginal center as part of their NAIDOC Week celebrations.

She might be a *somebody* at home and within her community, but at school she was a *nobody* — unpopular and a loner.

The other students made fun of her appearance. She wasn't a polished Instagram model, like the popular girls in her class. Her hair was usually greasy and hung in strings over her eyes. Her face was sprayed with freckles and her eyes, emerald green, had an intensity of someone beyond her years. And while most of the girls in her grade were now looking more like adult women, Dorothy remained stick thin and childlike. Her PE teacher remarked in front of the class one day that she looked like the girl who played Carrie in the original movie. The other students taunted her about this, even though Sissy Spacek was well before their time.

Dorothy made certain everyone knew she was Aboriginal. From the day she started high school she ensured she wore the colors of the Aboriginal flag every single day — whether it be a ribbon in her hair or badges on her jersey or her schoolbag. On plain clothes days she wore Aboriginal campaign t-shirts bearing slogans like *Tasmania has a black history* or *Justice and Rights.*

Every paper, poem or story she wrote, every project or assignment she worked on, had an Aboriginal theme. She steered class discussions back to Aboriginal issues and took every opportunity to correct teachers who used the words 'discovered' and 'settled' to describe the European invasion of Tasmania.

Dorothy's frequent trips to the principal's office were met with frowns and sighs from Principal White. Dorothy was a high-achieving student who didn't smoke, bully other kids, steal, fight or commit any of the other common school offenses. Her boldness in class was born from her unshakable passion for her heritage and her determination to set the record straight. At first, the school sent letters home to her parents, detailing her disruptive behavior. But her parents supported Dorothy's willingness to stand up for her beliefs, and so did nothing about it. Principal White could find no suitable punishment for Dorothy and resigned herself to just putting up with it.

~

'Looks like Dorothy's the only one then,' said Ms McGregor now, turning to the blackboard after surveying the class. Taking up a piece of chalk from the ledge below, she wrote *PALAWA* in large letters, and underlined it with a dusty swipe.

Dorothy put her hand down. Ms McGregor's words echoed what she already knew. She was the only Aboriginal. She glanced briefly at the rest of the class and then sat back in her chair, satisfied.

Until a voice from the back of the room said, 'I am too.'

'Well, well,' said Ms McGregor, smiling. She lowered her head and peered over the top of her glasses in the direction of the voice. Dorothy swung around in her seat, mouth agape. She recognized the voice. It was Amelia Davis.

When Dorothy was setting up the ASPA committee, she'd requested — or rather, demanded — that Principal White instruct the administrative staff to go through all the enrollment forms to retrieve the names of students whose parents had ticked the *Aboriginal and/or Torres Strait Islander* box. It turned out that there was a total of nine Aboriginal students enrolled at the school. Dorothy knew all but two of them through the Aboriginal community. She conducted a background check on the unknown two and both turned out to be legitimate. Of the nine Aboriginal students enrolled, Dorothy was the only one in her grade — a status that she took enormous pride in.

'Would you like to tell us about your Aboriginal connection, Amelia?' asked Ms McGregor. She shot Dorothy a smug smile and a raised eyebrow before directing her attention back to Amelia.

Amelia was one of the 'Princesses.' This was Dorothy's secret name for a group of attractive and mostly privileged students in her grade who hung around together and all wore a different shade of bright eye shadow in open contravention of school rules. Amelia was supercool and the group's unofficial leader. The color of her eye shadow was 'Tangerine Shimmer.'

'Well, I'm an Aboriginal … descendant,' said Amelia, turning to her friends and giving them a resigned shrug. 'I have Aboriginal ancestors apparently, which my father says makes me a descendant.'

The rest of the Princesses nodded their heads in support, their faces showing just the right degree of sympathy.

'A "descendant"? What is that supposed to mean?' snapped Dorothy. She'd pivoted in her chair so forcefully that she'd spun completely around and was now facing the back of the class, where Amelia Davis and the other Princesses' desks were lined up. The sincerity in Amelia's face was slightly betrayed by a faint smirk, and Dorothy knew that smirk was for her.

'It means you're not the only Aboriginal in the class, Dorothy, so please turn back around and face the front,' said Ms McGregor. Her eyes were sparkling.

Inside, Dorothy was screaming. As she turned back around, she gripped the base of her plastic chair so hard she felt one of her knuckles pop.

'P-A-L-A-W-A,' spelled out Ms McGregor, as she tapped each letter on the board with the meter ruler, 'is the word for Tasmanian Aborig—'

The lunchtime bell crackled through the PA system, cutting Ms McGregor off mid-sentence.

'Tasmanian Aborigines,' she continued, after the bell had rung out. 'Aboriginal studies are going to be taking us through to the end of term. See you all tomorrow.'

Dorothy was the first to leave the classroom, but she waited in the corridor and bailed Amelia up as soon as she came out of class.

'So, who is your family then?' she said, ignoring the other kids.

'Umm, why are you even talking to me, weirdo?' replied Amelia, looking to her friends with amusement.

'I want to know what your Aboriginal connection is,' said Dorothy. 'Who is your mob?'

'My mob? Oh. My. God,' said Amelia. 'My family is from Smithton. Like I said, Dad says we have Aboriginal ancestors or something and that's all I know.' Amelia lowered her voice. 'So why don't you run off to the library or wherever it is you go, you stupid … ugly … bitch, and mind your own business.'

Amelia and the other Princesses walked off, laughing to themselves.

'You're not one of us, you're an imposter!' Dorothy called out after her. She retreated to the ASPA room and threw her schoolbag onto the desk. It slid further than she expected and knocked over her mug, left from earlier that morning. Cold Milo splashed across the desk. The mug was her prized possession, made by her grandmother in her university art class. It was an imperfect black and emblazoned with an outline of Tasmania, filled in with the Aboriginal colors.

'Shit,' she said. 'Shit, shit, shit.'

'Language, Dorothy.' Cooper Jeffries, the librarian, entered the room.

'Sorry, Cooper,' said Dorothy, truly meaning it.

Despite Cooper being the librarian, Dorothy considered him a friend — her only real friend at the school, truth be told. He didn't fit the mold of most male librarians: he wasn't soft-spoken, nor did he have a beard. And he wasn't like the other adults at the school, either, who seemed to relish their authority over the students. Cooper was cool, she thought. He was a man who kept up with the times, unlike the other staff, who seemed so old-fashioned. He was tall and thin and had two full-sleeve arm tattoos — Japanese style. He kept his long black hair up in a bun and always underneath a black Stetson hat. The only thing about Cooper that wasn't modern was his taste in music.

Dorothy's first demand, upon getting the ASPA grant, was for the Aboriginal students to have their own meeting room. Principal White denied her request, saying they could use the school meeting room, but Dorothy wanted a room they could use all the time. It was Cooper who volunteered to share the library staff's common room with them. The room was rarely used by anyone anyway, he said, other than him. He took his breaks in there, listening to vinyls by King Crimson and Hawkwind. The rest of the library staff chose to use the main staffroom. Cooper's room had a small kitchenette and a large table, which, when Dorothy first moved in, was covered in piles of dusty boxes and books. There were no windows in the room and the lighting was dim. Dorothy had recruited some of the younger Aboriginal students to help her clean it up, and Cooper found another place for all the boxes. She'd tidied the room and put up some pictures and campaign posters on the wall. One of the pictures, taken by her father as a young man, was of a large group of Aborigines marching down a city street, carrying banners and placards and looking pretty rowdy.

Dorothy found herself another smaller desk, which she set up at the back of the room. The ASPA grant included money for a student computer, so one was purchased. It was on her desk and, although she allowed the other Aboriginal students to use it, they rarely did, so she quietly considered it her own. This was the place Dorothy came before school started, at lunchtime, and any other chance she could get. It was her sanctuary, where she was free from the bullying, the taunts and the childish pecking order. But more than a sanctuary, it was her office, where she conducted the business of the ASPA committee — and Dorothy took her role of chairperson very seriously.

She cleaned up the spilled drink, went to her filing cabinet and opened the second drawer, marked *Genealogy*. She removed all the files and spread them out across the desk.

'Some light reading?' Cooper glanced over Dorothy's shoulder at the assortment of folders.

'Yep,' said Dorothy, without looking up. She didn't have time for his small talk today. She only had forty-five minutes left of her lunchbreak to sort out this business with Amelia Davis.

The folders contained an assortment of family trees, genealogical reports, articles, legal papers and historical documents — all relating to Tasmanian and, in some cases, Australian Aborigines. Dorothy opened a folder labeled *Unsubstantiated claims*. Inside were documents on families and individuals who had claimed Aboriginality based on evidence that, as her mum would say, was flimsier than a silk diving board. She flicked through the folder and rolled her eyes at the ridiculous stories. There was one lady who based her Aboriginality solely on her belief that she could sense when blue-tongue lizards were close by. There were people who could find no ancestry whatsoever but just 'believed' themselves to be Aboriginal. There were a few families who based their Aboriginal identity on old family photos where one of the people 'looked a bit dark.' To them, that proved they were Aboriginal; forget about the various dark-skinned races known to have immigrated to Tasmania in the early days.

Dorothy felt herself getting distracted. She had already lost ten minutes. Smithton. Smithton was where Amelia said she was from: the north-west coast of Tasmania. Dorothy's experience guided her to two smaller folders. Within the first was a list of people who claimed to come from one of the daughters of a known Aboriginal woman who lived in the north-west and founded a large family. But the daughter in question didn't have any children. This group, many of whom originated from Smithton, had never been able to provide evidence of their Aboriginal ancestry, yet they continued to identify. Dorothy scoured the names for 'Davis' but couldn't find a link.

Inside the second folder were records relating to another dubious Aboriginality claim — also from the north-west region. It was based on a word-of-mouth story of unknown origins, involving a white woman who supposedly had a child to an unidentified Aboriginal merchant seaman in the 1890s. There were no archival records whatsoever corroborating the story — in fact, there were records proving this claim was false, but these families claimed to be Aboriginal regardless. Dorothy read through the material, careful not to miss anything.

'Ha!' exclaimed Dorothy, banging the table hard with her fist.

'Christ!' said Cooper, startled. He flopped into the nearest chair and put his hand over his heart.

'I've found it!' she said, triumphant.

'Found what?'

'Amelia Davis claimed in class today she was an Aboriginal descendant. And look here: a record of her family. An unsubstantiated claim, which means they are not Aboriginal at all. They are *imposters, fakes* — like I *fucking* knew they were.'

Cooper frowned at Dorothy's language. 'So what will you do now, Dorothy? Does it really matter?'

She shot Cooper a look of incredulity. 'Of course it matters. Does it matter if someone gives false details about their family tree in relation to a deceased will or trust? Yes. Does it matter to the police if someone gives them a false name or address? Yes. But everyone thinks it's fine to be sloppy about a heritage claim. With everyone wanting to be Aboriginal these days, that's a bad mix.'

'Fair enough.' Cooper put his hands in the air in mock resignation. 'Do you mind if I put some tunes on?'

'Knock yourself out,' said Dorothy. She was already packing up her documents. 'My work here is done.'

~

Dorothy turned up to social science class the next day with a spring in her step. She eyeballed Amelia Davis and the other Princesses as they walked in. Ms McGregor started the class by talking about the first European settlement in Hobart — at Risdon Cove — but Dorothy soon interrupted her.

'Excuse me, miss? Could we please continue our conversation from yesterday? I feel it was unresolved.'

'What conversation, Dorothy?' asked Ms McGregor, annoyed.

Dorothy turned around to look at Amelia. 'Yesterday, Amelia stated that she was Aboriginal. It is my understanding that she is not.'

'Oh, it is your understanding, is it?' said Ms McGregor. 'Face the front, please, and tell us how, exactly, you came to that conclusion.'

Dorothy smiled to herself. Things were going perfectly. 'I found Amelia's family tree,' she said, then turned again to Amelia. 'Is your father Gary Brian Davis?' she asked. 'And is your grandfather Brian Godfrey Davis, both of Smithton?'

Amelia hesitated. 'Ahh, he was. My grandfather died three years ago,' she said, glancing questioningly at Ms McGregor, who nodded back at her, as if to say 'wait.'

'Yes, I thought so,' said Dorothy. 'Your family is one of many that trace their Aboriginality back to a Mrs Eileen Waters, a white lady from the north-west who, as the story goes, supposedly had a child with an Aboriginal merchant seaman in the 1890s.'

The class was silent. Even Amelia had nothing to say.

Dorothy continued. 'Unfortunately, Amelia, the story doesn't hold up. You see, the fathers listed on the birth certificates of Eileen's children were all known white men.'

'What are you, the Aboriginality police?' accused Amelia.

The other Princesses giggled nervously.

'Enough, Dorothy,' said Ms McGregor.

'I haven't finished,' said Dorothy.

'I said *enough*!' yelled Ms McGregor.

The class went quiet. Ms McGregor walked to her desk, opened the second drawer and took out some papers. She flicked through them and pulled one out. She held it out to Dorothy and a crooked smile appeared on her face. 'You will like this,' she said, glancing at Amelia with a wink. 'This, class, is the school's Aboriginality policy.' She held it aloft. 'I asked the principal for a copy because I thought it might come in handy during our studies. It states here, class, that: *Aboriginal and/or Torres Strait Islander status is determined by self-identification by either the student, their parents or their guardian.* That is school policy. That means, everyone — and, in particular, you, Dorothy — that if Amelia, or anyone else for that matter, chooses to identify as Aboriginal, then that is enough for the school. We do not require any further clarification, and we certainly don't need students prying into the background of other students.'

'It takes more than school policy to make someone Aboriginal,' spat Dorothy. 'Aboriginal is something that you are. It is something you are born as. It isn't just something you can choose to be, such as a ... teacher. Or an idiot.' With her last words, Dorothy made a dismissive gesture toward the Princesses at the back of the class.

'Dorothy—' began Ms McGregor warningly, but Dorothy continued, speaking over her.

'Besides. The school's ASPA constitution says students must have Aboriginal ancestry and be recognized by the Aboriginal community before they are accepted as being Aboriginal.' She pulled the constitution from her own folio and waved it around herself, as Ms McGregor had done.

'And who wrote the ASPA constitution?' asked Ms McGregor, through gritted teeth. Her face was now red as a plum.

'I did,' said Dorothy. 'But—'

'To the principal's office, Dorothy.' Ms McGregor went to her desk and scribbled on a piece of paper. 'Take this with you. Go now.'

Dorothy's mind was racing. How could it have gone like this? She gathered her belongings, snatched the note from the teacher's hand and almost ran from the classroom.

She arrived at Principal White's office to find that she had already left for the day. Dorothy went, instead, to the library, to her office. She sat back in her chair and took a few deep breaths until her anger receded, allowing her to think more clearly. Then she fired up her computer and drafted an email to the Department of Education, highlighting the inadequacies of the school's Aboriginality policy. She cc'ed Principal White into the email. Dorothy read over the email a few times until she was satisfied. With a smile, she hit 'send' and left for home.

~

When she arrived at school the next morning, she headed straight for the library. She hadn't slept well. All night, she'd mulled over the events of the day, but by morning she'd convinced herself that everything would be okay. She might get a slap on the wrist from the principal, but she could wear that. It wasn't a major incident after all, and it wouldn't affect her grades. Walking up the stairs to the library she heard some commotion, and realized as she reached the top that it was coming from the ASPA room. Dorothy tensed up. That was her room. Some of the rage she'd felt the day before started to well up again. She dashed across the reading room and stopped in the doorway of her office. Inside, Principal White and Ms McGregor were talking to Cooper, who seemed agitated. The Princesses lazed on the chairs surrounding the large table. Some had their feet up on it. A few of Dorothy's folders were open on the desk, the documents spilling from them. The Princess with the green eye shadow had Dorothy's morning paper and was drawing devil horns on the people on the front page. Dorothy's vision brightened and became slightly blurry.

The principal noticed Dorothy's arrival and turned her attention from Cooper to her.

'Dorothy, from now on, any student who says they are Aboriginal, regardless of what you think, may be a member of the ASPA group and, as such, may use this room and its facilities,' she said, making a sweeping gesture with her arm. 'Furthermore, in a week's time there will be a new election for chairperson of the ASPA committee. Of course, you may stand for the position again.'

Ms McGregor grinned and indicated with a nod to the Princesses around the table. 'Although this time it looks like you will have a bit more competition,' she added.

On the far side of the room, Amelia Davis sat at Dorothy's computer. Facebook was open on the screen and Amelia was updating her status. She reached for a mug of Milo that was sitting next to the keyboard — Dorothy's prized mug — but knocked it over, spilling half its steaming contents onto the keyboard and the other half onto the floor. The mug fell too, breaking into pieces.

'Dorothy?' asked Principal White.

Dorothy didn't respond. Her eyes had locked onto the protest picture on the wall, where she was now staring intently, her thin body swaying like a flower on a reedy stem.

Dorothy was no longer in the room. It was 1977 and she was marching down the main street of Launceston. Just like in the picture, everything was black and white. The noise of the crowd was deafening. There was something behind the cries and the chants that Dorothy recognized: desperation mixed with nothing to lose. To her left was her grandmother, proudly holding up the Aboriginal flag. Around her were family — uncles, aunties, cousins. A big mob of blackfellas. Their banners said *Land Rights*, but what they really marched for was something unspoken: Recognition. Dorothy noticed the white people on the footpaths, all bared teeth and clenched fists. To them, Truganini was the last Tasmanian Aborigine, so who were these people? Dorothy felt at one with the marching crowd. She moved amongst them, with them. They didn't know where they were going exactly, but they had a purpose. They were moving forward.

Dorothy was wrenched from the scene by the sensation of being shaken. She was sprawled on the floor with Ms McGregor beside her, gripping her shoulders.

'You've had a seizure, Dorothy,' said Principal White, sounding far away.

Dorothy turned to look at Cooper. He had gathered all the pieces of her mug together on the table and was reassembling them as best he could. Bold, white cracks now intersected the Aboriginal colors like a tattered spider web.

'You'll never get that back together,' said Dorothy, her voice small and dull. 'It's too broken.'

'I don't know,' said Amelia, as she held one of Dorothy's Aboriginal flag t-shirts up to her chest and flashed her Tangerine-Shimmered eyes at the other Princesses. 'Nothing that a bit of superglue won't fix.'

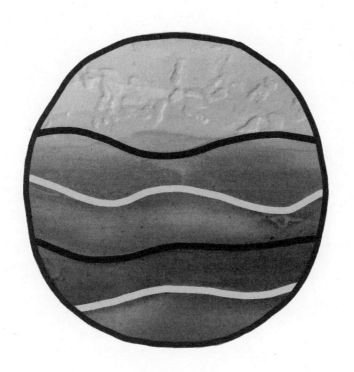

SONNY

On some winter mornings in Launceston, the fog doesn't lift until midday. Today it's so dense you can see the water droplets hang in mid-air, like rain in suspended animation. Crossing the car park, I turn the collar up on my leather jacket — a poor choice considering the cold and damp maybe.

At least it's black.

I have come out to farewell Sonny Burgess.

I spot Danny, Sonny's elder brother. He is a big guy, muscular. He looks out of place in a suit. Bluish tatts equally incongruous on the coffee-colored skin of his neck and hands. A bleach-blond girl, much younger than Danny, holds tight to his arm, sobbing like a runaway child come home.

'Shut the fuck up,' he says through tight lips. He stiffens his shoulder deliberately, jolting her head to the side. I experience an almost paralyzing wave of fear the moment he notices me. After what seems like a deliberate delay, he grants me one subtle nod before turning his glare back to the girl. His wife? Or his daughter, perhaps?

I breathe out, relieved. And scold myself for being such a pussy.

Our childhood relationships and experiences imprint themselves way longer than they should on our adult consciousness. Danny was a bad-ass and a bully when we were kids. Still is, from what I can see. His hawkish looks made him a hit with the girls, but to us boys they made him even more formidable. During early high school, on a sleepover at Sonny's house, Danny made me take off my sneakers and close my eyes. He directed me across their mottled front lawn until I walked in fresh dog shit. He made me stand on the spot while the crap squelched up between my toes. He threatened to smash me if I moved. Danny and his mates got a real kick out of it.

It was Sonny who pulled me away and rinsed my feet with the hose. Danny didn't say a word — he never did to Sonny. He looked after him. Cared for him. Everyone loved Sonny, it seemed. But he and Danny shared something special back then.

Special is the wrong word ...

Something dark and awful.

Their father was an abusive piece of shit.

I scan the crowd. The gathering is a mixed bag: elitist flash-blacks, common swamp riffraff, everything in between and any color you like. If there is one thing I've learned about black-fellas, it's that they're scarce when the cops are around — or Centrelink are on their case — but they'll come out in droves for a funeral.

I spot Kev, Sonny and Danny's estranged brother. He has his finger on the chest of the red-faced funeral director. Someone comes to the man's aid, and Kev backs off smiling, mouthing. Kev has a chip on his shoulder. Always has. When we were kids, we joked that it was because he was a ranga. The truth was, though, he copped a lot of shit from his family because he was fair-skinned, while the rest had a bit of color in them. It must have got to him, made him bad tempered.

Kev is the oldest. For some reason, he grew up with his grandmother. He called her 'Mum.' Everyone else called her

'Nan,' even me, before she passed on. She was a spindly lady with streaked, wiry hair. Spoke with an 'h' in front of her vowels. Always wore paisley and had a thing for brooches. A real clean freak too, forever scrubbing the floor. She lived in Invermay. 'The swamp,' we called it — an old cottage just a few streets away from Sonny's. Year round, that house smelled like mothballs and boiled vegetables. The family — Sonny's aunties, uncles and cousins — used to gather on her back porch in the summer, drinking long-necks and telling stories. The older boys would be off swimming at the gorge or hanging out at the York Park footy grounds, while Sonny and I hovered around the oldies trying to listen in. We'd eventually get the run. They didn't like us 'ear-wiggin,' they'd say. I didn't mind, really. All the stories seemed to revolve around 'birdin' or people Sonny knew and I didn't. Sonny hung off their every word. The stories stirred something in him. I could never understand it back then.

Sonny's father, Gary, was a real piece of work. I've often wondered why arseholes are blessed with such long lives. Must be some kind of joke only God knows the punchline to, because Gary's still around — these days he haunts the local nursing home where my ex-wife works. I don't expect to see him today. He's been a ghost for years.

To be fair, he had one or two good things going for him back in the day. Sober, he had an edge to him — something always simmering just beneath the surface — but he was a quiet man who tried to hold down a job. Unlike the rest of Sonny's family, he didn't mind us kids listening in. On his good days, he spoke about old times, about growing up on Cape Barren Island, going muttonbirding and the people he called 'the old fellas.'

Drunk, which he was more often than not, he possessed a cyclone-like rage that seemed to come out of nowhere and was as scary as hell.

Gary was mad keen on boxing, which matched up terribly with his drinking. He spent his younger days on the road with a traveling troupe, but he never made it as a pro. He tried to train the boys and was a pretty good coach when he wasn't charged up. Danny had the tough but lacked the grace. Sonny was the opposite — a natural mover and super quick. But Sonny hated fighting. Despised it. Ironically, he was named after Gary's favorite fighter: Sonny Liston. I'm sure the fact he hated the sport fueled Gary's rage toward him. But it was Danny who copped the brunt of the abuse. He protected Sonny, took the blame for any small slip-ups Sonny made at home.

'Dad's one of the stolen generation,' he told me once. I didn't get what he meant back then. I've come to realize he was making an excuse for Gary's behavior. Sonny never had a bad thing to say about anyone. He was like a ray of sunshine in the shadowy lives of those around him. People were drawn to him — I know I was. We fed off him like parasites.

His mum shot through just after he was born. Hooked up with one of her own, he said, referring to her white heritage. I don't think he ever thought badly of her though. I mean, who could blame her for leaving a man who blew his wage on piss and spoke with his fists. Sonny's Aunty Joyce sheltered him from his father through his toddler years. She was a nice lady who worked at the Aboriginal Centre in the early days — one of the pioneers. She was a fixture in Sonny's life up until a few years ago when the old pack-a-day finally caught up with her.

I can't remember the day Sonny started school. He turned up sometime during Grade One. But I remember the day we first met. It didn't take me long to notice we were nothing alike.

'Why are you brown?' I asked him. He just looked down and shrugged.

Another thing was that he spoke differently, said words differently. It wasn't unique to Sonny. His whole family spoke that way, especially his Nan. Now I recognize that it was the accent of the blackfellas — the ones from the islands — but as a child it was something exotic and it made Sonny special. (It also made him the target of persecution by the other kids, but that came later. And it was my fault.)

But differences don't really matter when you're six years old. They are what they are.

In fact, part of what bonded us in our younger years was that we *were* so different. My family life was easy. I was an only child. Dad worked for a shipping company in Low Head, operating the pilot boats that guided cargo ships through the Tamar River mouth. Mum was a dedicated housewife. We were by no means rich but we *were* privileged, I guess — looking back. Sonny stayed with us often, right through primary school and high school. He was quiet at our place. I think he appreciated the respite from his father. He never stayed for more than one night, though. He worried about Danny. Sonny loved to go out on the boat with Dad — we both did — and we often played around the gravelly shores at Low Head, making little fires amongst the rocks and cooking shellfish. Sonny knew the right ones to get, said that his Nan had showed him. They had another name for the Tamar River too.

They had so many names, for places, for objects. I couldn't pronounce them. It was like they had their own language, their own lexicon. I couldn't understand. I was always on the outside, trying to find my way in.

It wasn't until we started high school that our differences affected our friendship. It started when Gary took Sonny out of school for five weeks around Easter time and sent him to go muttonbirding with his aunty on Big Dog Island. I hated it, partially because I didn't get to go, but also because it was halfway through Grade Seven: a critical time, for me.

Sonny was my ticket to popularity.

He was good-looking and could run like the clappers, making him handy on the sports teams, and popular with the girls. When you're in Grade Seven that really matters. I needed Sonny, if I was going to matter.

When he came back from the trip he wouldn't stop talking about it. Suddenly, it was like being Aboriginal was the most important thing to him. I acted cool, but I resented it. I had worked out early that his family was unusual, and the word blackfella had been bandied around a lot, but never 'Aboriginal.'

Things came to a head one day on the footy field.

Sonny always got picked first. He could play football — by *God* he could. Watching him play and run like he did ... it was beautiful. *He* was beautiful. As strange as that sounds, everyone understood it. Even Gary — who blamed football for his son's lack of interest in boxing — was proud. He was the proudest man on the sidelines. Of course, he never said so, but you could tell. During practice one day we were picked on opposite sides. I was playing terribly and Sonny couldn't do a thing wrong. It was as if he was a magnet to the ball. Some of the other boys were getting frustrated too. I remember it all so vividly. I've gone over it a thousand times in my mind. Someone kicked the ball to me out of the square. It was a high ball and I was directly underneath. Sonny was in the right place at the right time and took a mark straight over the top of me, riding my shoulders and driving me to the ground. Any other day I would have shaken it off, but this day it had me fuming. Sonny hit the ground running and he was off with the ball.

In my frustration, I called out after him, 'Run, Darky, run!'

And run he did, and kicked another goal.

I didn't immediately regret what I had said. I was still angry. But my heart sank when the other boys kept up the chant — and more.

'Run, Darky, run ... Run, Abo, run.'

It's like we had all been so blinded by his coolness, his easy smile and his footy skills. We'd looked past his color, the strange way he spoke. The *muttonbirding*. But suddenly, in that instant, we shared a moment of clarity. In unison, we perceived the divide. He was Aboriginal. Sonny Burgess was a *darky*. To my dismay and shame, the name stuck. Sonny laughed it off, but we could tell he didn't like it.

The two of us never spoke of that incident and I didn't call him that again. I vowed that day to never again be cruel about his race. He was my best friend, and we remained that way right through high school. He still went muttonbirding every year, but I was no longer sore about it — that left me that day on the footy field.

Sonny ended up playing in the seniors. He was our hero. Practically a celebrity in the local footy circles. But the name stuck. It stuck. Whenever he got the ball the opposition supporters would call out, 'Run, Darky, run,' and then the laughter started. And other names. Worse names.

It got around that Danny handed out a few floggings over the *worse* names they used on his brother, so nobody had the guts to say those in front of him. It was my greatest fear back then that Danny would find out it was me who started it all.

Even as I spotted him just then in the car park, I realized I'm still scared.

Sonny got picked up by the AFL. We all knew he would. On his way to training one night in Melbourne, he was the victim of a hit and run and didn't walk again for twelve months. He tried to get back to form but he was injury-prone after that. Three years after being picked for the AFL, he was back in Tasmania again, playing local footy and looking for a job. I ran into him in town one day, not long after he returned. We hadn't spoken for a while, which was my fault. He'd reached out a few times during the height of his footy career, but my life was a shambles and I was jealous of his success, so I'd responded coldly. He eventually stopped calling.

'I started the "Darky" thing, Sonny. I'm sorry,' I said after the small talk petered out.

He just looked down and shrugged, like the day we first met.

'We were just kids,' he said.

They say that it's the ones you don't expect. I reckon that's true only about half the time. But never would I have imagined that Sonny would do what he did. Neither did anyone else, especially his brothers, who went on a rampage, desperate for answers. Was it financial? A woman? Somebody had to be at fault. After all, Sonny was a hero. He was miraculous. He was larger than life. In my mind, we were all guilty. We all wanted some of him to rub off on us. We all used him in our own way and we sucked him dry — me worst of all.

He never stopped giving, though. To me and to everyone. That was just what Sonny did. And when we no longer needed him, his job was done.

Sonny was my best friend. I made him feel small, that day on the footy field, attacking a part of him that was special, that he held sacred, and that made him who he was. And then I pushed him away when he made something of himself. Truth is, it was me who was small and insecure. I was the *darky*.

People are starting to move inside to the service now. From my pocket, I take out a pin in the shape of a muttonbird and in the colors of the Aboriginal flag. I poke it through the collar of my leather jacket. Another thing I've learned about blackfellas is that they guard their flag as a vestige of their identity. People look at the pin and then at me. There are a few frowns.

But today, I don't care. This is for Sonny. He would have liked it.

ABORIGINAL ALCATRAZ

I was crouching like a robber in the old tin bath, tipping water over myself with a pot, when a loud bang on the outside of the hut startled me.

Jamie's back, was my immediate thought. *Back from Flinders with some cold cans and the boat all nicely tied up and secure. Legend.*

I waited for the usual crunch of gravel and the double thump as he stamped his sandy boots on the splintery pallet outside the door. Instead came the clunk and jangle of a plastic bucket as it bounced and skidded down the hill, followed by a low rumble of thunder off to the west. A dense squall seized the hut. The shampoo wobbled off the driftwood shelf, splashing cold, milky bathwater into my face.

Shit.

I dried and slung the towel around my waist. My mind was sharp, now, with adrenaline. I had been on this island a long time — long enough to trust my senses when it came to the weather. As I stepped outside, the wind snatched the door from my hand and slammed it open against the cladding. Sand and dust blew in. One of my pet hates was a dirty floor and I'd swept it out with the rigor of a slave every morning and afternoon since starting the job. But now, as I looked up at the front rolling toward me, clouds low and moving fast in a long, black, churning line — unnaturally symmetrical — I no longer gave a fuck about the sand or the floor.

With a knot in my guts, I scanned the boat harbor and the open water between the islands. I couldn't see Jamie, as I had hoped, winding up the steep track on the tractor, arm draped around a carton of Boag's Green. The workmate I was responsible for, and my only companion on the island, was somewhere out on that sea. The rising tide had brought on the rollers, and they dashed the granite sentinels at the mouth of our harbor. White, foamy plumes — streaked with ribbon weed — rained across the coastal plains with the aid of the westerly, salinating thin soils and crystallizing the blue-grey cobbles above the beach. It was there, within that miracle combination of salt crust and sparse tussock grass, that the kanikung grew. It never failed to surprise me, even amid the distress and turmoil of this very moment, how it managed to survive, let alone produce the sweetest and most nourishing bush tucker.

Calm to violent; sweet to salty; alive to dead. That is the islands.

This duality, I had come to understand, was ingrained into this place; deep rooted like peat in a fine Scottish dram. And, just like whisky, the islands had a good side, but a bad one too. In this moment, I was seeing the bad side, and my brain was in overdrive, cycling through every possible scenario and returning to the worst ones.

The terrible ones.

The ones that iced up the marrow in my bones.

Over here, the weather got moody. Sometimes it wanted to kill you. I felt it right then, trying to send me back to the sea. All I could do was squint into the wind and shiver as the westerly drew the spit from my open mouth and replaced it with saline mist. My towel finally worked loose and sailed into the blackening sky, creating lunatic shapes on its jagged trajectory toward the distant blue hills of Cape Barren Island.

~

I stumbled back inside, wrapped myself in an old hospital blanket and placed my iPhone on the windowsill — the only place that got reception — and watched as one bar of signal appeared. The wall flexed as the draught ebbed and flowed under the door and through the gaps in the cladding. My ears popped. We made a mistake when we cut the windows in. It had compromised the strength of the wall. I called Jamie — once, twice, and again for good luck. Voicemail. I dialed the Flinders Island Pub. I knew the number off by heart.

'Mike, it's Ray here from Chappell Island.'

'Who?'

It was my idea to do the grog run. I knew Jamie would be keen. He'd been jonesing for a beer for the last few days. This afternoon, when he dropped the chainsaw a bit too hard and screamed 'Fuck you!' to nobody in particular, I could tell he'd reached the end of his shit. It had been a long week of hard work. I loaded the gun when I mentioned how nice a beer would be after work. He gave me a look that said he would do it, and I gave him a nod that said he could. Then he was gone. A quick scan of the ocean had shown calm, relaxed water; the only movement was the tide rippling through the channel between this island and the next. And daylight saving meant there was enough light to get home. Now this.

'Yeah, Mike. It's Ray, from Chappell Island. One of the Aboriginal—'

'Oh, yeah, Ray — how's it going out there?' Mike half yelled above the din of the jukebox. In the background, a woman yelled for ten dollars on *Imperial Jack*, for a place.

'Yeah, okay. Is Jamie there?'

There was a pause and some muffled speaking. I closed my eyes and hoped this meant he was putting Jamie on the phone.

'Sorry, Ray, the punters are on fire tonight. Who were you after, sorry?'

'Jamie.'

'Jamie ... Jamie — oh, one of your fellas. Yeah, he was here earlier.'

'Is he there now?' I cleared my throat to disguise the desperation in my voice.

'Nah, he left a while ago — maybe an hour. With a carton and some rollies. Said he was heading back to Chappell. Look, it's pretty noisy in here ...'

'Yeah, I can hear.'

'You boys gonna fix your tab up soon? It's getting up there.'

I held my phone in front of me and squeezed it. There was a cracking sound and the screen went blank. The bastard chooses *now* to ask about our goddamned tab? I tapped the display and it lit up again. 'You there, Mike?'

'Yep.'

'I'll fix that up next week.' I ended the call and expelled a long sigh before trying Jamie's number a few more times.

Fuck you, Jamie. Answer.

Reaching for the marine radio that was mounted on the wall near the window, I realized my hand was shaking.

'Calm down, ol' boy,' I said out loud, being careful not to depress the button on the side of the handpiece. It looked like a sharp key on a piano. The channel dial rolled between my thumb and forefinger, reminding me of a woman's nipple.

I found some momentary comfort in the numb, toneless clicking of the dial as it turned. I watched the tiny screen. The red segmented lines of digital numbers rearranged themselves in a chaos that was hypnotizing.

I stopped on channel sixteen: the emergency channel.

As I put the mic to my mouth, my bottom lip started to quiver. I noticed for the first time that I had been laboring for that deep, satisfying breath we don't realize we take until we can't get it. I hadn't felt like this since I was a kid: the involuntary meltdown. The feeling that you are losing it.

I stood motionless for a while, willing myself to make the call. Once you contacted the emergency services, there was no going back. Once they were notified, it was on record. It was against work rules to use the boat for anything other than work, and that included going to Flinders Island for grog. In fact, the rule had been made to *stop* people going to Flinders Island to get grog. Until now, we had always got away with it. Mike the publican wasn't going to tell. He'd be doing himself out of business. Ours was a dry island and a dry program, but a beer or two after work reminded you that you were there of your own free will. Made you feel human. Those who had actually been to jail compared working on the island to a stint. It was tough: the physical work, the isolation, the rules.

I put the mic down, went to the window and scanned the ocean again, as if giving it my attention would bring Jamie back safe. It didn't.

~

I knew Jamie had had it tough growing up. He was the youngest of many siblings, barely registering as a blip in the lives of his tweaker parents. When he was first sentenced to the youth detention center for stealing cars, he was too young to be part of the Rum Island program. Once a kid turned fourteen, they had the choice of the detention center or Rum Island. Black kids, that is. They usually picked the island because they took it as the easier option. They weren't locked up. They had the run of the place. It wasn't security fences that kept them in, it was the sea. 'Aboriginal Alcatraz,' they called it. Jamie had upgraded from stealing cars to burgin' houses, and he eventually got done. He was fifteen and a half when he went to court. This time, he chose the island. I was working on Chappell Island at the time, building a tractor shed for the workers. I'd had visits from the Alcatraz boys a few times. They came up with the program worker in the boat. One time, they knocked off all my squid jigs. Another time, it was a full packet of smokes. After that, I learned not to trust them.

Their program coordinator, Bernice, wasn't suited to the islands. She was a burned-out office worker, trying her hand at a lifestyle job. The boys broke into her cabin once and found the keys to the fuel store. Bernice caught them in there, sucking on a forty-four. The way she described the kids that day made the whiskers on my neck itch: all of them standing there, swaying, with a ring of rust around their mouths, eyes focused on something unseen. Petrol sniffing was serious business, and the policy in this situation was to call in a plane and send them off. But Bernice was scared of losing her job, so she didn't report it. Instead she sent them to their rooms that night with a warning. The next day they all did a shit in the small water tank feeding Bernice's shower. She knew there was something wrong from the smell, and her suspicions were confirmed by the bits of corn she found floating in the tank.

When Jamie came to the end of his second stint on Rum Island, the mob that ran the detention program sent him to work with me. Of course I didn't want it — but I had no choice. To my surprise, he was suited to working. He helped me finish the shed and then we started on the weed work together. We'd been here ever since — the two of us. He stayed here now, by himself, when I went to town for my days off. He'd come a long way, but still didn't trust himself in the city. Other workers came and went. It's a hard job and a tough environment to live in, but Jamie had found a place here. I'd taught him everything I knew about the islands — about boats; about our history — and he took it all in. The juvenile offender was gone. The islands had claimed him. He was a stand-up young man, hungry for his culture and a legitimate dollar in his pocket. Here, he had become a somebody. But a dead somebody becomes a nobody again pretty quick.

~

I put the radio handpiece back in its cradle. Calling it in meant explaining why Jamie was out in the boat. Once it was called in, my employer would be notified, which meant I would lose my job. Of course, if Jamie died or was hurt, it would mean more than losing my job. He was my responsibility, so I'd probably go to jail. Worse still, I'd have to face his family — and the rest of the Aboriginal community.

Fuck that. I'd rather die myself.

I looked out the kitchen window at the mountain the whitefellas call 'Mount Chappell.' Our fellas call it 'Hummocky.' It seemed to have magic properties that made it attract rain. There was no rain falling on the tin roof of the hut, yet it swept across the mountain like a ghostly veil. I pictured the newborn water carving out tiny rivulets in the granite sand, as it followed the path of least resistance down the mountain and into the lowlands. All that water then made its way out into the sea, to where Jamie was.

One last look, and then I'll make the damned call.

Realizing I was still naked under the blanket, I threw on my storm gear. I white-knuckled the doorknob this time, as I left the hut, and managed to push the door closed behind me. I leaned into the wind as I climbed the hill. A twister broke loose from the ocean and ripped its way across the plains, dispersing loose vegetation and dust in spiraling fountains. The long grass and coastal shrubs along the sides of the track had succumbed to the wind and lay crippled and straining against the ground.

I fought my way to the base of the mountain and headed west, to get a view of where Jamie should pass around the island in the boat. On a good day, he would be home by now. But this squalling westerly would be cutting across his bow, the waves smacking him on the diagonal. He would be forced, constantly, to steer the boat into the waves — hitting them head on. Then, to maintain his course, he would have to maneuver back toward the island in between the waves in a constant zigzagging pattern. Outside the lee of the islands, the waves would tower over the boat, their crests churning and ragged. And white. The color white. In all manner of cultures, beliefs and spiritual systems, white is a healing color. It is pure; it is wholesome. It is life. But not for ocean-goers, and not for us blackfellas.

Oh, no.

White makes you wary. White equals death.

And when you are navigating the breakers, white is what you avoid.

I skirted the mountain, sheltering my face from the rain and debris of the storm. I kept moving until I could see across to Whitemark, the township of Flinders Island. Jamie would be traveling from there. Things were much worse on this side. My visibility — looking into the wind, rain and dust — was limited enough, but to spot a small tinnie out in the raging ocean ... that would be almost impossible. A few times, I thought I glimpsed the boat. My heart and my hope rose and fell in my chest like the waves. I kneeled down beside a rock and stared and stared until I could barely see the water. After nearly an hour out there, and in the very last light of the dying day, I prayed. For the first time since I was a child, I prayed to God: God, who I didn't even believe in. And I wept.

~

I didn't even stamp the mud from my boots. I didn't even turn on the light. The marine radio was sounding out from its corner by the window, illuminated by the evil red glow of those numbers that taunted me.

'Sécurité, sécurité, sécurité ...' The repetition of this word meant that a marine safety warning was about to be given. Stumbling back from the other side of the island in the dark, I had come to the final and awful conclusion that there was no hope for Jamie, or for me. Jamie was dead — smashed up against a reef somewhere, or flung from the boat and drowned. This meant that my life was over too. No job. Disgraced. Shunned by my community. They would all know it was my fault, see it as my fault. The people who were proud of me for looking after our islands. The Elders I had always looked up to. My shame would be reflected in their eyes.

As the announcer read the weather warnings, in his perfectly timed and measured voice, a realization gripped me with such panic that I fell to my knees. What if Jamie wasn't dead? What if he was clinging to a rock somewhere or grasping the edge of the capsized tinnie — pleading eyes searching, desperate for the lights of a helicopter that his best mate and mentor on Chappell Island must have called? He would have called it, right? Any good man would have called it in, as soon as the storm first hit.

And the worst thing was that I still couldn't bring myself to do it. Hope was so far away now. Lost. The whole world was lost. The radio announcer's voice trailed out and then he was gone too.

I banged my head against the wall. Hard. The pain felt good, so I did it again with more force. The dizziness it brought was sublime, welcome. A hard gust hit the wall and something toppled from the windowsill and landed next to me. My phone. The screen was illuminated and a message icon flashed in the corner. In a daze, I swiped at a hot gush of blood coming from my forehead. I opened the message. It was from Jamie. I smeared blood across the phone's screen and squinted through the red streaks at the words:

Hey man. Missed your call. Was just getting the boat out of the water. Weather came in so I'm staying on Flinders. Beer is going down well. See you tomorrow.

~

I woke on the floor, sometime in the night.

After reheating the water, I crouched like a robber in the old tin bath and scrubbed the dust and dried blood from my face and hair. The hut was no longer shaking; the storm had died out. With the radio now turned off, there was an incredible silence — and the peace it brought was an old friend I hadn't seen in years.

I thought again about the kanikung growing down by the salty shore and about the strange duality of the island. And, suddenly, came an irresistible desire to walk down there in the dark and rip off a ripe bud, just to taste its sweetness.

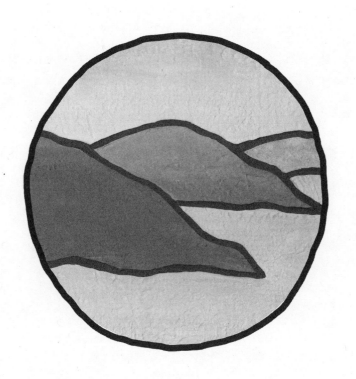

BLACK EYE

I lay awake last night, thinking about the worst thing I've ever done. The memory came on a tide of negative thoughts. This happens to alcoholics. Regularly. Some call it 'alcohol anxiety' or the 'grog demons.' To me and to other blackfellas I know, it's the 'black eye.' I can't decide if it's a blessing or a curse that our brain tries to make life bearable, for a time, by suppressing all the bad stuff. All I know is that when we're back in the gutter — when things go to shit — it all comes flooding back. Yeah, that black eye is a real bitch.

Now, the worst thing I have ever done.

A big statement, I know, for a fifty-year-old man who has lived a full life. And there's plenty who'd give you a different opinion about what my 'worst thing' was. But what's it matter what they think, right? I'm the one who has to live with it.

I blame Hardo, partly. It was his gun, after all.

'Check this baby out,' he said, with a roguish grin, as he unrolled the oily rag from where he'd hidden it in his swag. There's no way they'd have let him on the boat knowing he had a gun. It was an air rifle — .177 caliber — with a barrel so bent it was like it had an elbow. The steel of the gun was orange with rust and the wooden stock was gouged and splintery. It was the most busted-arse gun I had ever seen, and I strongly doubted it could even fire.

It was Hardo's first stint on Woody Island. He arrived a day earlier with three other blackfellas rounded up in Launceston by a Landcare group who had money to employ Aboriginal people. They were promised a few weeks' work on the islands, cutting and spraying weeds. Truth be told, I was glad for the company. I'd been on the job for over a month. Just me and a lazy bastard, Mansell. We were always at it — me and Mansell — because he was such a bludger. By the time the others came, we hadn't spoken for days. In my eyes, Hardo seemed the least promising worker of the bunch. He was the youngest of the new guys, straight black hair, combed back with product. A real city slicker. Built like he hadn't done a stitch of physical work in his life. Completely out of place on the islands. I put fifty mental dollars on him being the first to get shitcanned.

I was conscious of my age, thirty-seven at that time, which I felt was old for having my first run as supervisor. So I took things pretty seriously. As soon as those boys jumped off the boat, I gauged their worth as laborers. I planned on working them hard, you see. Hardo looked hungover. He winced as he collected his pack and swag. As he trekked the rough track to the work hut, he spewed in the long grass.

But he didn't say a word, the whole way there.

The others were friendlier — all handshakes and greetings. Billy and Aaron were brothers from down south. They were both burly guys, and bouncing with enthusiasm. When I saw their nervous glances at the beach and grass around them, I felt the warm glow of satisfaction. They'd obviously heard the tales of the Woody Island copperheads. Mansell noticed too, and he tried to set them at ease, saying the snakes were docile this time of year. In that moment, I hated him more than ever.

'Why'd you bring a gun over here, Rick?' I asked, as he passed it around. He wasn't Hardo at that stage. His nickname evolved, over that first work trip, from Rick to Riccardo, and then to Rockhardo, before settling on Hardo. The name suited him, in a funny sort of way. He thought of himself as a hard man, with his swagger and his tales from the streets. But the more you got to know him, the further you could see through his bluster. Hardo stuck, as a joke name, really — but he loved it.

'I dunno. Shoot stuff, I guess.' He found a dented International Roast tin in his bag and shook it.

I assumed, from the dull rattle, that it was full of pellets. 'Well, we don't kill things over here, man,' I distinctly recall saying. 'We're Landcare workers. We're supposed to look after the place, not blow the wildlife away.'

'And you 'specially can't shoot the birds, ol' man,' said Mansell in his Cape Barren Island drawl. 'They're the old fellas, you know? The old people — watching over us.'

I felt like slapping the black off his face. I'd been listening to his airy-fairy spiritual shit for the last month, and I was over it.

'Do you have a *problem* if I set up a target?' asked Hardo, looking squarely at me. His chin jutted out in challenge.

'In your own time, fine. But if anyone gets hurt, it's on your head.' I felt like I was backing down a bit, but I didn't want to seem too overbearing. I didn't want an us-versus-the-boss situation.

Over the next week, the job took over, and I forgot about the gun. We burned off all the dead gorse plants that Mansell and I had cut and dragged into piles. And we cut and sprayed new ones. Billy and Aaron worked like troopers and were easy to get along with. They argued amongst themselves a lot, though. Billy — the younger brother — was constantly stirring Aaron, and we all got a laugh out of it. Even Mansell, the lazy bastard, seemed to come back to life.

Hardo was in a bad mood most of the time, because he wasn't allowed to use the chainsaw. Everyone else had a chainsaw ticket, but not him. Billy started calling Hardo 'poison boy' because he had to do the spraying. It caught on, and everyone razzed him up. Hardo hated it. He challenged Mansell to a fight during smoko one day. I reckon he thought Mansell was the weakest. I had to step in and give Hardo a warning. He spat on the ground at my feet and walked away.

We had some free time on the weekend and the crew were scratching for things to do. Billy took an empty bottle of White King down the hill from the hut. He set it into the side of a large pile of dry gorse, about sixty meters away. Hardo brought out the rifle and the tin of pellets. The crew started taking shots at the target, but they struggled to hit it. I watched them for a while. They were having a good time, even Mansell was having a go. But I could see that they were aiming straight at the target, not taking the bent barrel into consideration.

Against my better judgement, I said I could hit it. Hardo turned to look at me. I could see his mind ticking over. He didn't want me to show him up. He'd been trying to undermine my authority with the crew. He was trying to destabilize us.

'No way you can hit the target. You couldn't shoot your way out of a fucking bag,' he scoffed.

Without a word, I reached for the gun. Hardo held on to it for a moment, before reluctantly giving it to me. I crouched down in the gravel and cocked the mechanism. Someone had sprayed canola oil on it, and it snapped back together with an easy click. Rifle loaded, I propped up the barrel with my left hand and snuggled the stock into the right side of my chest.

'Go, boss,' said Aaron.

Hardo shot him a look. I could see how the barrel was bent to the left, and slightly up. I adjusted my aim to the lower right side of the target. I fingered the trigger.

It had been years since I'd shot a gun. My first time was with my stepfather, on the bank of Brumbys Creek. I was eight years old. We were duck shooting, and he let me fire the 12-gauge into the willows on the other side. The recoil knocked me on my back and I was winded. I cried, and my stepfather jerked me up by the arm. He wiped the tears from my face with his rough hand, before any of the other shooters could see.

'Fuck you, Dad,' I whispered now, and fired. The pellet blew the top off the bottle and sent it spinning away. The crew whooped and cheered.

Hardo swore and kicked at the dirt. 'What a fluke,' he said.

'Fluke, was it?' I looked back at the target and then winked at the others.

'Try and hit something else, then,' said Hardo. 'Something further away.'

At this point, I know I should have called it quits. I'd upstaged Hardo, and put him in his place. But I wasn't satisfied with just driving the knife in — I had to twist the blade.

'Like what?' I asked.

We looked down the valley, toward the water. On top of a large boulder, something white stood out against the blue backdrop of the sea. It was about eighty meters away, near the beach. We all saw it.

'That white thing, on the rock,' said Hardo.

I squinted down the barrel of the gun and lined the object up with the sight. At this distance it was featureless. It was the right size for a bird, but it wasn't moving. I took a long time to steady the shot. I think I was waiting for Mansell to tell me not to shoot it; not to shoot the bird, because it was one of the old fellas. But he didn't and, with his silence, I was condemned.

I aimed low and to the right — and fired.

The white thing on the rock disappeared.

I felt a shock go through my body. Tendrils of dread spread through my chest.

'I think he hit it,' said Billy.

'He did!' shouted Aaron.

'Let's go and have a look,' said Hardo.

I thought he'd be gutted that I'd hit the target, but he wasn't. He had perked up and was striding down toward the beach. We all followed. I tried to get in front, but Hardo walked fast. I prayed to the universe that I hadn't killed a bird. I knew Hardo was praying that I had.

We reached the rock. It was tall. At least fifteen feet. There was nothing at the base of the rock, or off to the sides. It must have been a bird, and it must have flown off the rock at the sound of the gun. I started to feel relief.

Then Hardo's voice came to me. 'Round here, at the back,' it said.

My lungs constricted. My mouth went dry.

'Holy 'taters,' I heard Mansell say.

I walked around behind the rock.

On the ground was a large white eagle. A trickle of red stained its robust, grey-streaked chest. I picked it up. It was surprisingly heavy, and warm and limp in my arms. I willed it to be alive, but it didn't move. I had killed countless muttonbirds in my life, but that was different. Birding is in my blood, part of my culture. The death of this eagle was another thing altogether. Only minutes earlier, it was proud, majestic. It probably had a partner, perhaps young ones to care for.

The enormity of what I had done weighed down on me, and I felt hot tears well up in my eyes. Conscious of showing weakness in front of the crew, I turned my back to them and laid the bird on the ground. I can't even remember what I said during those moments.

Hardo was the first to speak, and his words, and their timing, were perfectly executed. If I wasn't so devastated, I may even have admired him.

'I can't believe you killed a beautiful sea eagle.'

'It was your fucking gun, you … prick.' My accusation came out as a hopeless whine.

But they were already walking away. All of them together, with Hardo in the lead.

The next day there was a fire on the island. That morning we'd been burning off a pile of dry gorse. During smoko, while we were in the hut, a westerly picked up and the fire spread through the dry grass. It moved quickly across the flats and up one side of the mountain. I'd hardly spoken to the crew all morning, but I managed to call them into action. I knew I had lost their respect. Once news of what I had done reached my employers, or the authorities, I expected to lose my job. And now, with a major fire on the island, I was done for.

'It's because you killed that eagle,' said Mansell, as we ran out to fight the fire.

I didn't reply. I wanted to feel anger toward him, but I couldn't. I knew he was right. He had been right all along, and I didn't listen. Besides, anger seemed to be missing from my emotional repertoire that day. All I could feel was sadness and regret — then, and for a long time after. Looking back, I think that lack of fury was a good thing for me, at the time. It didn't last, though.

Hardo ended up with the supervisor job. But, of course, that's what he always wanted. Maybe that's why he brought the gun in the first place.

It took a while for the fury to find me, for it to settle like a cold bullet in the chambers of my heart.

It's still there. Most days, I can ignore it. But in the grip of a terrible hangover, when the black eye opens up, it comes to life within me. And I wonder, then, which old fella it was who I killed. I wonder how much of my life, after that day, was shaped by that action.

But most of all, I wonder what would happen now if I got my hands on another gun. A straight one. If they let me back on that island.

Hardo still works there, you know.

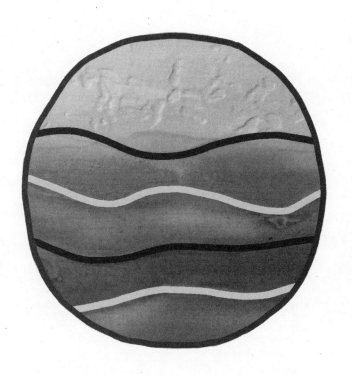

THE BLACKFELLAS FROM HERE

The brass plaque read: *The owners acknowledge that this house stands on Aboriginal land.*

It was neatly fixed to the brickwork by the side of the doorbell. The house was an impressive three-story on the edge of the Launceston CBD. Fairytale windows, set into a gabled roof, provided a million-dollar view of City Park. The front yard was surrounded by a high brick fence, and in a green pond by the path leading to the front door, there stood two smiling, moss-covered cherubs — frozen in eternal glee. The house screamed old money.

'Rich bastards,' said Kat to herself, as she walked up the steps and onto the porch. Turning back toward the pond, she flicked the smouldering remains of her cigarette at one of the cherubs. It bounced off the concrete eyeball and fell into the water with a hiss.

A week earlier, the house had featured in the real-estate guide of the local newspaper. One of the photos had been a close-up of the plaque. The owner, Dr James Clifford — a prominent psychiatrist from Launceston — had been reported as saying that, *he and his family hoped others would follow suit and provide similar gestures to the Aboriginal people, both past and present.*

Kat pressed the doorbell and a gong resounded from deep within the house.

Within seconds, a silhouette appeared in the glass panel in the door. The outside light came on, and the door was opened by a man in his mid-fifties, who was cradling a half-filled brandy snifter. He wore a maroon cardigan, neatly pressed slacks and a pair of worn but expensive-looking house shoes. His black hair — grey at the temples — was wet and slicked back, as if he had just showered. A spicy scent wafted off him, accompanied by the unmistakable smell of roast meat from inside the house.

The man lowered his head slightly and squinted at his visitor over his glasses. 'Can I help you?' His voice was calm and pleasant. Kat immediately pegged him as a schmoozer.

'Good evening, sir. Are you James Clifford?'

'Yes, I am. Why?'

'I was hoping I could talk with you about something.'

James looked his visitor up and down, his eyes taking in Kat's lithe figure. He took a sip from his glass and leaned against the doorframe. 'Well, we're about to have dinner. Are you selling something?' he asked, with a wink.

'I'm not selling anything, Mr Clifford—'

'*Doctor* Clifford,' he interjected. He gave Kat a lazy smile, like someone who knows they will impress.

'I was hoping to talk to you about your plaque, Doctor Clifford.'

'Ah yes, I've been getting a few questions about that lately. What would you like to know?'

'My name is Amy,' Kat lied. 'I'm a student at the university and I'm doing a paper on Aboriginal land return. I was hoping to ask you about what motivated you to install a plaque acknowledging that this is Aboriginal land.'

'Okay, well, I suppose I can answer some questions, ah … Amy. Come in. If you don't mind, I'll eat my dinner while we talk?'

He held the door open for Kat to enter, and she did.

'Don't worry about taking your shoes off,' he said, taking in her high-top Doc Martens. 'There's enough lace there to rope a sail.'

The house was warm and the smell of meat was stronger inside, making Kat's stomach growl. She pulled her backpack from her shoulder and followed James's gesture to head toward an open door up the hall. The clanking of kitchenware sounded down the passage.

'Sorry if this is a bad time,' said Kat, turning back to James. As she did she saw his gaze lift from her arse.

'Please wait in my office, I'll just finish up in the kitchen,' he said.

Kat walked into a room lined with red-cedar paneling. A crammed bookshelf took up one corner, and an open fire crackled on the far side of the room, next to a mahogany sideboard. In the center of the room was James's desk, neatly arranged. A green banker's lamp provided the only light in the room other than the fire. She sank into one of two red chester-fields in front of the desk and placed her backpack on the floor. She closed her eyes and ran her palms along the smooth, cool leather of the armchair. It smelled like paper money.

A woman's raised voice from the kitchen brought her back to reality, along with the loud bang of a ceramic plate being put down a little too hard. James appeared at the doorway with a tray of food and a glass of red wine. He sat on the business side of his desk and started his meal. The manner in which he ate, Kat thought, made him look grotesque: his dry, manicured hands held the shiny cutlery as delicately as a surgeon, yet he slopped the food into his mouth like an invalid. Somehow picking up on her distaste, he dabbed at the corner of his mouth with a napkin, removing the streak of gravy that lingered there like a brown, translucent slug.

'So, what do you want to know about the plaque?' he asked finally, putting down the napkin and reaching for his wine.

'Why is it there?' she asked, almost snapping at him. She saw James raise an eyebrow and checked herself.

'What I mean is ... What is the reason you had it installed?'

'Well, many years ago—' James began.

'Ah, wait ... if you don't mind, Doctor Clifford,' interrupted Kat. She reached into her backpack and took out a handycam attached to a short tripod.

His eyes narrowed. 'You never mentioned you were making a video.'

'If you don't mind,' said Kat, setting up the camera. She placed the tripod on the desk, facing it toward a sheepish-looking James, who moved his half-eaten dinner to the floor.

'I don't see why you need to film this,' he said. 'You said you were doing a paper for school?'

Kat watched him through the viewfinder. 'It saves me from having to make so many notes, Doctor Clifford. And if you could just stay in roughly that position throughout the interview, that would be great. Thanks.' A beep signaled that she had pressed record.

James smoothed out his cardigan, then produced a comb from his slacks and ran it through his hair.

'Let's start again, shall we?' Kat asked, without waiting for an answer. She mouthed the words *three, two, one*, and then continued. 'So, Doctor Clifford, you have had a plaque installed at the front of your mansion. It acknowledges that this house is built on Aboriginal land. Can you please explain why?'

James cocked his head at Kat's use of the word *mansion*, and shot her an inquisitive look before answering. 'Well, there is a bit of a story behind that,' he began. 'Many years ago, I did some work in a remote Aboriginal community in the Northern Territory. It was after I finished my psych residency training in Sydney. Cyclone Tracy had just gone through Darwin, and many of the Aboriginal people in the affected areas were left without anywhere to live. Those homeless ones surged into the outer communities, which became overcrowded, creating terrible living conditions. The Feds put a call-out for doctors to go there to aid the people; meds to deal with the disease, and psychs to deal with the grief and loss. I was hungry for experience so I jumped at the chance. While I was there, I met someone I'll never forget. He wasn't a victim of the cyclone. Raymond Chong had grown up in the community that I was working in and, even at his young age, he was a respected community leader. Ray became my counselor during my time in that community and, when I think back, I'm sure he helped me more than I helped any of his people. If it wasn't for Ray, I think I would have run away from there, screaming.' James paused in reflection for a moment.

'Anyway, three years ago, the AAP — that's the Australian Association of Psychiatry, by the way.' He pointed to the wall behind him where a framed, silver-leafed certificate hung. 'They held a conference in Darwin, and I was invited to be a keynote speaker. After the conference, I drove out to the community that I had worked in, all those years before, to see if I could find Ray. The community had been replaced with a uranium mine. The whole area was fenced off, and there was security patrolling — no doubt to keep the Aborigines out. I went to the nearest town and asked about the people who seemed to have simply disappeared. Most people didn't know anything, but one of the Elders I spoke to said that the people from that community had moved on. Many had come to the town, but they fought with the locals, and so they left. I never got to see Ray again, or learn of his fate — or that of his community.'

James reached for his wine but checked himself when he remembered the camera was rolling.

'Anyway, we moved to Launceston from Sydney in '95, and we bought this house. This *mansion*, as you call it. I started to consider what happened to the Aboriginal people who once lived here, you know? I read that the people from this area were either killed or forced away from here very early during the settlement of Tasmania. I figured that, although the circumstances were different, it was the same outcome for Raymond and his people. The uranium mine stands as a reminder that their land was taken, and their community destroyed. I suppose this house — and the other buildings in this town — stand as a reminder of what hap-pened to the Aboriginal people of Launceston.'

'And that is why you had the plaque installed,' finished Kat.

'Exactly.' He folded his fingers together across his chest, leaned back in his chair and fixed Kat with a self-congratula-tory smile.

After a moment, Kat reached into her bag and pulled out a manila folder, which she placed on the desk and opened. She drew a neat bundle of papers from it and slid them across James's desk.

'What's this?' He picked up the papers and flicked through them.

'They are conveyancing papers, doc. They've been drawn up by a lawyer.' She paused. 'This is how you sign your house over to the Aboriginal community of Tasmania.'

James looked from Kat to the papers. Then to Kat again. 'What the hell are you talking about? Is this some sort of j-joke?' His face contorted.

'No joke,' said Kat. She tapped the papers with her index finger. 'There's an asterisk on every page that you need to sign and initial.'

'There's no way on Earth I'm signing this place over to you, or anybody!' said James through gritted teeth. 'And you don't even really look that Aboriginal by the wa—'

'I'm offering you an opportunity to put your money where your mouth is, doc,' Kat interrupted. 'You have publicly acknowledged that this house stands on Aboriginal land — with your fancy newspaper article, and your trendy plaque out there.' She gestured with her thumb toward the front door. 'And now you've poured your heart out on camera, with your ridiculous

sob story about the "Great Raymondo" and his disappearing—
reappearing community. What this comes down to is that if this
house stands on Aboriginal land — and it was wrongly taken, as
you say — then here is your chance. You get to right the wrongs
you speak of, and give your house and your land back to us: the
blackfellas from here.'

James, slack-jawed, slowly rose from his chair.

'Sit down, doc. I haven't finished.'

He sank down again.

'Oh, really?' came a female voice, startling both of them.
James's wife stood in the doorway. She spoke with a breathy drawl.

'I can handle this, thanks, Darla,' said James, snapping back
to reality.

Darla Clifford stepped into the room with a slight sway. She
was tall — at least six foot. In one arm, she cradled a miniature
Chihuahua, its face snuggled into her powdered cleavage. With
her other hand, she carried a wineglass in her fingers, the way
rich people do. Some of the wine sloshed from her glass onto
the carpet as she walked, and she rubbed it in with her foot.

'Sorry about that, James,' she said, laughing to herself.

'Get out of here, Darla,' he said, almost pleading.

His wife ignored him and sat down on the edge of his desk.
Her tight satin dress rode up her smooth, tanned legs, revealing
to Kat a glimpse of Hello Kitty underwear. Darla didn't bother
adjusting it. Kat knew she wanted her to see that, even at her
age, she had it going on.

'We are doing an interview,' said Kat, with a scowl. She was
not just annoyed at the interruption — she was also perplexed
by Darla's choice of undies.

'No, lovey,' said Darla. 'What's happening is that my husband
has been picturing you naked for the last ten minutes, while you
have been trying to stitch him up on video so, presumably, you
can show the world how clever you are.'

'Is that what you think I'm doing?' Kat said. She was over the surprise of Darla's entrance now and back to her cool, calm self.

'Well, why else would you be here, lovey? You don't seem as desperate and lost as the women James usually lures into this room.'

Shaking his head, James sat back in his chair and drained his wineglass.

'Well, I'm glad you're here,' said Kat. 'This involves you too.' She picked up the handycam and moved it to the mantelpiece, so that she could fit Darla into the frame, and cleared her throat.

'All my life,' she said, 'I have witnessed upper-class white people — like you two — getting all the breaks. Living in nice houses, driving flash cars, kids in the private schools. All the while, my mob — the blackfellas — we have to live in the shitty parts of town. Always trying to scrape by on the bare minimum.' Kat checked the red record light on the camera.

'It has pissed me off no end, this … injustice. This land used to be all ours, the resources all ours. But now we live like paupers in our own country, while you people shamelessly flaunt your privilege and wealth.'

Darla closed her legs and smoothed out her dress. She put the Chihuahua on the floor and it ran straight to James's plate and devoured the remains of his dinner. Darla moved across to the sideboard and poured herself a neat whisky.

'But over the years,' Kat went on, 'I've made my peace with this situation, like most of my mob have. Life goes on. Our organizations do their best to get a better deal for us, but very little changes. And it's always the way, isn't it? The most down-trodden people — they complain the least about their lives. It's because we don't have time to. We're too busy trying to survive, trying to make ends meet. Do you know why most blackfellas don't bother voting?'

James lost his cool and, standing, slammed his fist down onto the table. 'Who gives a shit? I've heard enough,' he said, rubbing his hand. 'I won't be lectured and spoken to like this in my own home. We've entertained you long enough, I think, young lady. Now take your damned camera and leave, or I'm calling the police.' James placed his hand on the phone at his desk.

'For God's sake, James,' said Darla, sighing. 'You invited her in here, you old letch. Didn't you learn your lesson after the last little slut sued you out of my holiday money?'

'Shut the fuck up, Darla!' spat James. 'You're making this worse. And anyway, who are *you* to call me *old*, huh? You're no spring lamb.'

Darla stumbled toward James's desk, her last few drinks clearly catching up with her. She poked a finger at his chest, in mock authority. 'I'm in better nick than *you*, Mr Floppy.' She almost collapsed in a fit of laughter.

'Yeah, go and have another drink, Darla,' said James. His face had turned a peculiar shade of red. 'You haven't peed yourself yet.'

'The night's still young, dear.' Darla went to the mantelpiece and picked up a crystal prism inscribed with frosted lettering.

'To Mr Award-winning Psychiatrist ...' Darla said into Kat's camera. She held up the award and pretended to read the inscription, her voice starting to slur. 'For prescribing yourself a record amount of Viagra.' She set herself off into another laughing fit.

'Right, that's it,' snarled James. He turned toward the fire, where the dog had settled, and patted his knees with both hands. 'Tiddles, good dog. Come here, girl,' he coaxed. Kat could hear him trying hard to conceal the anger in his voice.

'Leave Tiddles alone,' responded Darla, her laughter subsiding.

Obedient, the dog scurried over to James, who seized her triumphantly. He lifted her up by the loose skin on her neck and held her, cocked, over his shoulder. A shocked and shivering Tiddles whined. Her little feet pawed at the air.

'I'm going to throw Tiddles into the fucking fire if you don't get the hell out of my office,' said James. His manner was strangely calm, but his expression said *just try me*.

Darla, eyes wide, drew in a deep breath and fell to her knees.

'Man,' said Kat to herself, 'this is gold.' She was watching the scene through the viewfinder of the handycam, which she'd picked up as the argument had progressed.

'I'm serious, Darla. Leave now and I'll put Tiddles down.'

'You're going to pay for this,' slurred Darla, getting slowly to her feet with the aid of the desk.

James and Kat watched in silence as Darla stumbled out of the room. Even Tiddles stopped whining for a moment. James put the dog down onto the floor and it scurried back to the fire and lay there shivering, its beady eyes fixed on him. He put his head in his hands for a moment, before looking up and into the lens of Kat's handycam.

'And you're still here,' said James with a sigh.

Kat smiled and nodded. 'That's right. And, doc, you won't be calling the cops. In fact, I want you to throw that *phone* into the fire, right now.'

'Why should I?'

'Because I have all this on camera. Including the part where your wife revealed your infidelity … oh, and the part where you threatened criminal animal cruelty.' She laughed and rolled her eyes. 'You act so woke, Mr Clifford, don't you? Despite your privilege, you're a real bleeding-heart man of the people. But privilege doesn't make you a decent human being.' She cocked an eyebrow. 'Clearly.' After a pause, she said: 'And who uses a landline these days anyway?'

He yanked on the phone cord and the plug sprang from the wall, then he tossed the phone into the fire without looking. It landed in the coals, and made a defeated beeping sound before it burst into green flames.

'As I was saying,' said Kat, 'like most in my community, I had resigned myself to this situation. You're the *haves*, and we're the *have-nots*. I mean, what can I do about that, right? But what really irks me — what really gets my goat — is when whitefellas, like yourself, run with this tokenistic bullshit. Example: the plaque at your front door. And it's not only these plaques, either. What's with these *acknowledgement of country* speeches that kick off every public event these days? *It's all just words!* Where is the action? If you acknowledge that this is Aboriginal land, then bloody well give it back. Don't just say it, do it!'

'I don't know what you want from me,' he replied. His shoulders were hunched over, and he looked to Kat as if he had shrunk somewhat.

'What I want, doc, is for you to sign this house over to the Aboriginal community, and then I will leave. Sign the papers and I'm outta here.'

'Even if I sign the damned papers, they won't be worth a cracker to anybody,' hissed James.

'We'll see.'

'Once the authorities are made aware that you are black-mailing me—'

'I'll still win,' said Kat, 'because you'll see your own hypocrisy every time you open your front door.'

'These papers will be null and void,' finished James.

'Look at you, *invader*' — she opened her arms to encompass the stately room and ostentatious wealth — 'relishing in the spoils. You're no better than that fucking mining company. Now sign.'

He shrugged and then flicked through the documents in front of him, signing at the required places. The only sound aside from the scribbling of his pen was the occasional pop and hiss of the melting telephone. James reached the last page and then slid the papers across the desk to Kat, who scooped them up with one hand and shoved them, along with the handycam, into her backpack.

'Good dog,' said Kat, smiling. She reached down and gave Tiddles's disproportionate head a tousle. The dog didn't take its eyes off James.

Kat poured herself a short whisky from the sideboard and downed it in one go. 'Thanks for the hospitality,' she said.

'Fuck you,' replied James, and gave her the finger.

'I think you will find our contract gives you twenty-eight days to vacate the premises. But, considering your generosity, I'm sure we can manage an extension, if you need one.'

The clap of Kat's Doc Martens on the hallway floorboards carried through the now-silent house as she made her way out. James's last words came as she closed the door behind her.

'Don't think you've got away with this. This will be all over the news.'

Kat stepped out into the cold, lit a cigarette and watched the smoke cloud rise above the garden. 'Well,' she said to the two cherubs on her way down the path, 'it better be.'

YOUR OWN ABORIGINE

'God, Jonesy's a prick,' said Matt. He placed a crumpled pack of Longbeach on the bar then stared at his hands, palms up. Blisters that had formed, burst and then formed again wept at the base of each finger.

'Well, he *is* the boss,' replied Jay. His gaze didn't move from the TV above the spirits shelf, which showed the grainy highlights of an old AFL match. 'Being a prick is a quality all bosses have — 'specially in our game.'

Matt winced as he brought his beer to his lips, expecting pain, but the icy glass gave his hands relief. He took a long swig and followed it up with a satisfied, 'Ahhh.'

'But I agree, he could have got a digger in for that trench. I mean, we're bricklayers, for Chrissake. They have machines for that shit. We're not in the Dark Ages.'

'Yeah, and even if Jonesy *couldn't* get a digger in there, he still could have got me some help. I dug that whole foundation myself. By hand.' Matt held up his mangled palms to emphasize the point. 'He got Craig and that other dickhead laborer to do a friggin' Bunnings run — *and* pick up his smoko. And didn't they milk it too? They were gone for over two hours.'

'I don't know why you bother whingeing about Craig,' said Jay. 'We all knew he would get it easy, when Jonesy put him on. Craig's his sister's kid for fuck's sake — and you know what Kath's like … she's a bloody mole.' Jay turned to the bartender and raised his empty glass.

'Didn't stop you shagging her,' teased Matt, a hint of smile puncturing his sullen mood.

'Righto, righto,' said Jay, trying hard to conceal his own smile. 'That was ages ago. And anyway, she kinda looked alright back then.'

'Maybe, but she was still a mole.'

'Yeah, well, it had been a while, so … you know, any port in a storm.'

'I still wouldn't have … hey, hey — check this out, will ya?' Matt indicated with a nod to the door.

Craig entered the bar alone. 'Look at you two bums,' he said, as he strode up to the bar.

Unlike Matt and Jay, who were still in their hi-vis shirts and stubbies, both spattered and streaked with mortar, Craig had been home. He was showered and dressed for a night out, in a brown leather jacket over a white t-shirt, casual jeans and brown leather shoes. Shiny. He pulled out his wallet — one of those crocodile-skin ones popular in the '80s, also shiny — placed it on the bar, then nodded to the bartender. She answered with a smile and suggestive tilt of her hip.

Matt made a show of looking Craig up and down. 'Nice out-fit, cock,' he said. 'Didn't know you were a wog.'

'Stop hating on me, bro,' said Craig, checking out his reflection in the mirror behind the bar. He wrinkled his brow into a faint scowl, giving himself the James Dean look. 'It's not my fault you had to dig that trench today.'

'That's why we have laborers, *bro*. So, they — you — can do the shit jobs and we can get on with *our* work.'

'Come on, you fellas,' said Jay, staring at the TV. 'Work's over. It's Friday, just forget about it.'

'I agree,' said Craig, settling himself onto a bar stool.

'Yeah, you would—' began Matt.

'Hey, can you please turn that up'? Jay called to the bartender.

'Sure, love.' She picked up the remote and aimed it at the TV. The image of a newsreader with shiny, black hair and too-red lipstick burst into life. The caption below — the one that had caught Jay's eye — read: *Sponsorship Bill causing an uproar.*

'*With the opinion polls showing the Liberals are down two points from last week,*' said the newsreader, '*the Prime Minister is touring the country — no doubt trying to soothe the discontent caused by the extreme changes the Liberal Party has made to Aboriginal welfare. Reporter Murray Inglis is in Melbourne, where several of the major unions have convened a rally, denouncing the changes. Are you there, Murray?*'

The shot changed to a street scene in the Melbourne CBD, where hundreds of angry people were marching down a crowded inner-city street, chanting and carrying banners and union flags.

'*Yes, Noy. Thanks. We're here in Flinders Street, where all the major unions have organized a demonstration against the Aboriginal Welfare Bill that was passed through federal parliament almost six months ago to the day. Nicknamed the "Sponsorship Bill," the new law has generated a huge outcry from both Aboriginal and non-Aboriginal groups across the country.*'

'Turn that shit off,' came a raspy voice amongst the crew at the eight-ball table.

Jay elbowed Craig, who whistled to the bartender and pointed to the ceiling. She got the message and turned up the volume.

Matt continued to stare at his hands, dabbing at the blisters with a green serviette. On the TV, the shot changed. Now the reporter was standing on the edge of the street as the protesters surged past. Someone threw a water bottle, narrowly missing him.

'The most controversial aspect of the new law,' the reporter continued, staying composed, *'and the part receiving complaints from both sides is the compulsory sponsorship of Aboriginal welfare recipients. The blame is being attributed to the rise of the ultra-right-wing Australia for Australians Party, who received an unprecedented number of seats in the federal election and joined the Liberals to form government. Under the new law, Aboriginal welfare recipients — those Aboriginal people receiving any form of Centrelink payment — must be personally sponsored by an Australian taxpayer. This is a radical move by the Australia for Australians Party, who say that Aboriginal welfare is a huge burden on the economy and that most taxpayers are oblivious to the money wastage. They say tax dollars go into one large bucket that provides no accountability.'*

'Your round, wog-boy,' said Matt. He pushed his empty glass toward Craig.

Craig looked at his own beer, which was still over half full. 'We're doing rounds?'

'Shut up, you two,' said Jay. He felt for his wallet and put it on the bar. 'Next round's mine.' He turned back to the TV.

'A party spokesperson says that, under the new system, taxpayers will know exactly who their money goes to, and how it is being spent,' the reporter continued. *'The government is coming under fire for targeting Aboriginal people. Their response is that welfare dependency is significantly higher amongst the Aboriginal population. The suspension of the Racial Discrimination Act was a necessary action, they say, not unlike what happened during the Northern Territory intervention several years ago. There are rumors that the government will extend the law to all Australian welfare recipients in the future, but nothing has been confirmed. Aboriginal communities across Australia have condemned the move, saying that it is racist and demeaning. A raft of lawsuits and High Court actions are currently pending, and the expected outcome is unclear. For now, the current policy stands. Back to you, Noy ...'*

'Switch the fucking thing off,' yelled a guy standing at the jukebox.

Craig stood up to protest but was cut short by Angus Young ripping into the opening lick from 'Thunderstruck.'

The bartender shrugged and Craig sat back down.

Jay turned to Matt. 'So, have you got yours yet?'

'I have,' Craig interrupted, before Matt could answer. He opened his wallet and pulled out a card like a driver's license. Smiling, he slid it along the bar toward Matt.

Jay intercepted it and held it in front of him, studying the picture. It showed an attractive young woman. She had tanned, even skin and a large smile, showing straight, white teeth. A pleasant face. The card didn't show her address, but it did state that she was from Bowraville, New South Wales.

'Oh, nice. Did you get a letter with it?' asked Jay.

'Sure did,' said Craig, beaming. He took a folded piece of paper from his wallet and opened it. Jay could see that it was typed on a computer and signed by hand at the bottom in pink, glittery pen.

'Her name is Davina. She is seventeen and a half. It says here that she grew up in Bowraville and she has just received a scholarship to go to university in Sydney. She says my money will assist her to study to be a registered nurse, and that she plans to come back home when she finishes the course, to work in her community.'

'Ha. You got a good one too,' said Jay.

'Certainly did, bro.'

The bartender arrived with three beers. 'You boys comparing dicks?' she asked with a raised eyebrow.

'You'd think so,' chimed in Matt, sulkily. 'The way they're carrying on.'

The bartender rolled her eyes at Matt and gave Craig a wink, before sliding off down the bar to pull beers for the other patrons.

'Check mine out,' Jay said, flashing his card toward Matt, who looked away in disgust.

Craig leaned over for a closer look. 'Christ, she's ... kinda old.' He was unimpressed.

'Maybe, but look at this,' said Jay. He unfolded a letter from his wallet, similar to Craig's except that Jay's was entirely hand-written. 'Her name is Barbara and she lives here in Launceston.'

'No shit,' said Craig. 'You got a local!'

'There's more. Barbara billets kids who come off the islands to go to school in Launceston. She says here that my money goes toward looking after those kids. She currently has four of them living at her house — one of them plays footy for North, in the under-sixteens. I'm going to watch the girl play next week-end at Aurora Stadium. Apparently she's AFL good.'

'You guys are sick,' said Matt. 'Look at yourselves, will ya? Gloating over "your Aborigines." It's bullshit. Why should we work our arses off so that they can have an easy life? It's not fair.'

'It's no different from how it was before,' said Craig. 'It's not like any more money comes out of our pay. We still get taxed the same amount, but at least we know where it's going — well, some of it anyway. What the government do with the rest of it is the bloody travesty.'

'Ooh, it's a *travesty* is it, Craig?' said Matt. 'Fuck me, it doesn't make any difference. The problem hasn't changed. If they're gonna give our money to the blacks, it should go to improving education and training, so they can bloody well work like the rest of us. What did they use to call it ... "Closing the Gap"?'

'They tried, but it didn't work,' said Jay. 'We all know why this Australia for Australians Party did this — to make us resent blackfellas — but I don't think it's working. Most people that I know are happy with the Aborigines they sponsor.' He took a sip of his beer and shrugged. 'I mean, you hear the odd story of someone getting a dud, but mostly people are happy, I think. I know I am. Like Craig said, it doesn't cost us a penny more than it did before, but now we can see where our money goes, and I'm proud of how mine's being spent.'

'Yeah, me too,' said Craig, holding up his beer for a 'cheers.' Jay accepted and they clinked glasses.

'So, who did you get then, Matt?' asked Jay. 'Did you get a fizzer, did you?'

Craig burst out laughing at Jay's choice of words.

'No, I didn't,' said Matt sharply. 'I haven't bloody got one yet, have I? And I don't want one neither.'

'It's compulsory, mate,' said Jay. 'The government will send you one anyway. You're in the right tax bracket.'

'Well, I'll send the bastard back then,' yelled Matt. He stared down the other two, challenging them. 'And I don't want to hear any more about it.'

'Righto,' said Jay. 'Calm down, ol' boy.'

Matt swiped his cigarettes off the bar without a word and walked out to have a smoke.

When he was out of sight, Craig jumped off his stool, went to Matt's spot at the bar and opened the wallet lying there.

'Hey, what are you doing, mate?' asked Jay.

'I bet he *has* got one.'

'Yeah, but you shouldn't be going through his—'

'Look, see!' Craig pulled a card out from Matt's wallet and held it up, triumphantly. 'He does have one!'

Jay glanced toward the door. It would take Matt at least a couple of minutes to have his smoke. He might even have two, considering his mood. Jay snatched the card off Craig, and swiveled the other way on his stool so Craig couldn't see it.

'Hey, let me see!' Craig looked over Jay's shoulder.

The picture on the card was of a man who appeared to be in his mid-thirties. He had a big, cheeky smile and one of his front teeth was missing. The man was wearing a battered Akubra and was holding something up to the camera. The object had been blurred out but, from the color and the shape, it was obviously a beer can. A VB can, to be exact. The name on the card was William Pony and he was from Darwin.

'Holy shit,' gasped Craig, slapping his leg. 'Matt *did* get a fizzer.'

'Looks like it,' said Jay. He turned back toward the door. 'Check if there's a letter.'

Craig searched through the wallet and found the letter. It was handwritten and smeared with red dust. He opened it and read it out aloud:

'Hey, bloke, I wish I could say I'm sorry that you got me to sponsor, but I can't. Sucked in, I reckon. It's people like you that vote for these crooked politicians. This dickhead from the government came out to my town to see me. Took my photo and all and made me write you a letter, which I'm doing now. My sister girl is helping because my spelling's no good. Reckon that's because they closed the school here in my community when I was young. They closed all our schools back then. Said there was no money but they kept them open in the city, where all the white kids were. Anyway, I don't have much to say. I'm going to use your money to buy beer and smokes when my royalty cheques run out. We get those monthly, you know, from the mines near our community where they diggin' up all our country. We can't go there anymore cos there's a big fence. You took our land. Reckon it's fair enough you buy me a beer. William Pony.'

Without a word, Craig put the card and letter back in Matt's wallet.

When Matt walked back in, there was a fresh pint waiting for him.

'Yeah, that Jonesy, eh?' said Jay, looking over at Matt's hands and shaking his head. 'You're right, mate. He *is* a prick.'

They didn't talk about 'their Aborigines' again. Not that night, and not ever.

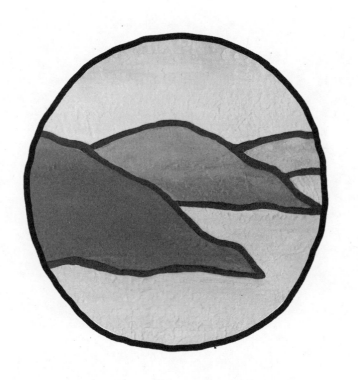

BLEAK CONDITIONS

The park was like a scene from a Jack the Ripper movie. The trees were backlit by an amber haze, and the shadows sloped at a curious angle. Jarrod skidded across the frosted mud and grass as I dragged him by his coat. His arms hung limp against his sides, and I sensed that, if he tripped, he wouldn't have held them out to break the fall. The indifference he displayed toward his own wellbeing made me wince. I had expected some of his usual bullshit, but I hadn't expected him to act so broken. From his coat, his clothes and his hair there emanated a nauseating blend of sweat, campfire smoke and cheap cooking sherry.

There were other people in the park too, crowding in. I refused to look at them, banishing them to my peripheral vision. I pictured their soiled hands, outstretched toward me — fingers cupped, reaching, wanting. I blocked out their voices with a loud hum. I refused them everything: no recognition; no storage in my brain for their image, their detail. A figure blocked my path. I had time to stop, but I raised my arm instead. Something softened under my elbow. The thud that followed and the accompanying whimper betrayed no gender. I laughed at how politically correct it was.

'You didn't have to do that,' said Jarrod, once I'd bundled him into the car. He spoke in a monotone, his features expressionless.

I was reminded of myself as a child, sulking after being told off by my parents; punishing them, for as long as I could hold out, with my utter lack of interest in everything. Closing myself off.

'What the hell, Jarrod? Three in the goddamned morning. You asked *me* to come and get *you*, for Chrissake.' I shook my head. I had let him rile me up. I had promised myself that I wouldn't allow him to do that. It always ended up like this.

'I meant, you didn't have to hit my friend.'

I let the car speed into the next corner. The tires squealed, and fear-lines patterned Jarrod's face. I started to calm down. But I couldn't let his comment go.

'I didn't hit anyone. What are you talking about?' I said through a yawn. The car had a taxi-like ambience, and it was making me tired.

'Didn't you?' He looked at me for the first time. His head moved slowly, like he was stiff and in pain. 'So, T-rex broke his *own* nose, did he? Knocked *himself* to the ground, did he?'

I felt myself getting pissed off, but this time I embraced it. When you're trying to keep yourself awake, anger is the equivalent of winding down the window.

'Hey! I didn't *hit* anyone. That … that dero got in my way! He, she — whatever it was — should've stayed out of my fucking way. I mean … *T-rex*? Really?'

'You're an arsehole, man. You haven't changed at all. I shouldn't have called you.'

~

The garage door lowered behind us, and the internal light flickered on. I expected to have to pull him from the car, but he was out before I was. He half stumbled through the garage, peering at my stuff and nodding his head, as though he was reaffirming something in his mind. He ran his hand along the bumper of my jet ski, and then pulled it away fast. It was an exaggerated motion, as if he'd been caught with his hand in the biscuit tin.

I heaped some sheets and blankets on the couch. Susan and I called it 'the rack,' because lying on it destroyed your back. I figured it would be fine for Jarrod though. He should be used to couch surfing by now. I heard he'd been sleeping in the park, of late — 'The Square,' as they call it — opposite the Aboriginal housing co-op in town.

'Have a shower,' I said. 'There's a spare towel in the bathroom.'

He didn't respond. Instead, he flopped onto the couch and flicked the stained collar of his German army surplus coat over his face. He didn't even take off his boots. The pile of bedding slid onto the tiles, where it stayed until morning.

~

'Daddy, Mucka Jarrod is here,' announced Seth, my sunny four-year-old. He bounded onto the bed, exuding the kind of glee only children can.

As I rubbed at my eyes, he landed on his knees between my legs, missing my groin by inches. I instinctively rolled into a protective position. Two years ago, we had all laughed when Seth's first stab at 'Uncle' came out as 'Mucka.' The name stuck. Jarrod liked it because he reckoned his nephew was naturally nonconformist. He refused to accept otherwise. His world view was that when Aboriginal people digressed from societal norms it was a form of protest against colonization. He called it 'cultural deviance.' I called it a bunch of bullshit.

'Mucka Jarrod stayed the night.'

'Did he, boy? That's cool. Hey, what time is it?'

~

When I came downstairs, Jarrod was at the kitchen table. His dark curls were slick and damp from the shower. He had on a pair of gaudy board shorts, and a white surf-brand hoodie. Seth ran to him, and Jarrod scooped him up affectionately.

'Wassup, black boy?' he asked the writhing mass in his arms.

The furrows of my brow deepened. 'Black boy?'

'Yep. He's like us, bro.' Jarrod pulled up Seth's singlet, showing his brown belly. Seth, thinking he was in for a tickle, covered up, wailing. Playfully, Jarrod scruffed a handful of Seth's dark curls. 'Look at his hair. He's a spit, out of your mouth.'

'Where'd you steal the threads?' I asked, with more than a hint of derision. I wanted to steer away from the subject of our heritage. It always led to an argument.

'Um, honey?' Susan called, from the back of the kitchen, 'I was going to tell you, but I let you sleep in. I gave Jarrod the clothes I got you for your birthday. I didn't think you'd mind. I'll get you something else.'

Amongst the breakfast items on the table was a bunch of tags. Susan had a habit of leaving price tags on presents, so that people could admire her generosity. The tag from the hoodie said *$179.95*.

'Fucken hell,' I blurted out.

Jarrod's fork squealed as he stabbed at the last of his bacon.

'Honey, can you not swear around Seth,' came my wife's voice, this time from the laundry.

'Sorry, bub,' I called back. 'Sorry, boy.' I tousled Seth's ringlets. 'Don't listen to Daddy.'

'That's good advice,' said Jarrod, not looking up from his plate.

It had been a year and a half since Jarrod had been in our home. My family loved him — everybody did. Except, it seemed, for me. We had a sour bond, past our use-by date. We always had. Mum blamed me, said I'd been jealous when he came along. Said I'd been too long an only child. Maybe she was right. Maybe that's the reason I'd been putting off the second-child discussion with Susan.

'We need to talk. Tonight,' I said, under my breath, so my wife couldn't hear.

'Yeah, whatever,' he replied. 'And don't worry about the clothes. I won't take them with me.'

I looked at the congealed yellow streak down the front of the hoodie, where he had slopped egg yolk.

'Nah,' I said. 'They're yours now, cock.'

~

Jarrod agreed to look after Seth in the house, so Susan and I could spend the day working in the front yard. After Seth's third escape, I came inside. Seth had dragged a dining chair over to the door and let himself out.

'I thought you were looking after him.'

'This Netflix has some alright shows,' said Jarrod. 'Even if they *are* corporate wankers who ruined TV.'

Jarrod had retrieved (or made Seth retrieve, more likely) all the pillows from the bedrooms. He had combined them with the couch cushions to make a soft throne for himself, where he sat watching television in one of my old singlets. He flicked a piece of Lego across the room at Seth with his big toe.

'Don't get too comfortable,' I muttered into a tumbler of water.

'Ay?'

'I said, put a shirt on, will you? You've made a sweat stain on the couch, and I can smell the grog coming out of your skin from here.'

~

The evening meal was pleasant. We made pizzas in the wood oven outside. I stretched the dough, while Susan helped Seth put on the toppings. Jarrod managed the fire. He handled the peel like a master, revolving the pizzas smoothly with a quick turn of his hand. It was impressive, and my dark sentiments toward him lightened. He told us a story I'd heard many times, of working in a pizza restaurant during his jaunt through Italy — a 'real pizza joint,' he emphasized.

Jarrod had been hit by a car when he was seventeen. He was drunk and tried to jump over a plumber's ute. It was his fault, but he got a payout anyway. He backpacked around the world for two years on that money.

Jarrod appeared to be enjoying the evening, especially with his nephew hanging off him — his 'protégé,' he claimed, trying to provoke me. But I noticed that there was something underlying his mood, something slightly desperate in his eyes. He was struggling to hold it together.

'Can I get a photo of you boys?' asked Susan.

We lined up in front of the oven, with the dragon tree to one side. Jarrod held the peel like a guitar, and Seth clung to his neck. Susan indicated, with a flick of her head, for me to move in closer. After an awkward pause, I placed my hand on Jarrod's back and then slid it up to his shoulder. My fingers cupped the hard ridge of his clavicle. The movement brought us together, and I felt his body against mine. It was curved and racked like an old, arthritic street dog — all hips and distended joints. In contrast, I was soft from my office job. Those nights on park benches, stony garden beds and concrete stoops had taken their toll on my brother. He was only thirty-seven. I tried to suppress a pang of guilt, but it prevailed: I had made him sleep on our shitty couch, knowing what a bastard it was.

He fixed me with a solemn stare. Seeing something in my eyes, he turned back to the oven and started sweeping out the firebricks. I felt he could sense a moment of weakness in me and was trying to exploit it. I hated the suspicion he aroused in me — and not just the suspicion. All the feelings, not one of which was good. I had been rehearsing our 'talk' all evening, but I still wasn't prepared. I had no idea, really, what I was going to say. But I knew I didn't want to talk to a drunk.

Earlier, while working in the garden, Susan had said, 'Why don't you tell him he can stay with us? I don't mind, as long as he sorts himself out.'

'What's the point of trying again?' I replied. 'We don't get along. We never have.'

Jarrod put down the peel. 'You got anything to drink?'

~

'Here you go,' I said, pointing the cap end of a bottle at Jarrod.

He was sitting outside on the patio table, constructing a rollie. He took the beer with a grateful, yet dubious, nod. He sat with it unopened in his hand, waiting for the catch.

'Drink up, then,' I said, and took a swig of my own.

'Cheers,' he replied, and downed the whole stubby.

'This is healthy, you know,' I started hesitantly. 'Just a *couple* of beers ...'

'I don't need a lecture on drinking, bro. I'd rather leave.'

'Yeah, right. And go where? Back to the park?' I instantly regretted saying it, and the tone that I'd used.

'Can I have another beer?'

I sighed. 'Why not?'

Jarrod went to the fridge and grabbed two more stubbies. Before I could tell him that mine was still full, he put both of the bottles down in front of himself.

'I know you're going to tell me to sort my shit out,' he said. 'But I'm going to tell you first: you need to sort your own fucking shit out.'

'Hey. Quit fucken swearing,' I said, through gritted teeth. 'Seth—'

'Is inside, so shut the fuck up,' Jarrod finished.

Rage incapacitated me, and I couldn't reply.

Into the silence, Jarrod continued, 'You're in denial.'

'Denial?' I laughed, mockingly.

'Yeah, denial. And you're living a lie.'

'Okay, Jarrod, Mr Scholar of the World. What's this lie, then?'

'You're in denial about your Aboriginality, and you're living like a white man.' He spoke matter-of-factly.

'Oh, here we go. The "black and white" thing, again.'

'Look around,' he said. 'Look at this house — it must be costing you a fortune. Every tool and knick-knack in the garage, every piece of crap that you just *had* to buy, but never use. A ridiculous *jet ski*.'

'You're on a roll, mate. Keep going.'

'A mortgage, which you're locked into for life. *Life*, bro. And a fucking trophy wife. I mean, Christ, I love Susan — she's a better person than you are — but you couldn't have gone much whiter.'

'Don't bring Susan into this. The way I live my life has nothing to do with my heritage. And it's got nothing to do with you either, for that matter.'

'We're palawa, whether you like or not. I hate it that you live like a raytji. It brings shame on me. Shame on our community. I want my nephew to grow up proud of who he is.'

'Shame?' I was fighting to keep my voice down. 'Coming from someone who lives in the park? I'm the one who should be fucking ashamed. My brother sleeps with T-rex and the other losers in The Square, living on free coffee and stealing staff lunches from the fridge at the bloody housing co-op. Youse are a frigging *disgrace*.'

'At least I'm with my people,' said Jarrod. He had taken on a sulky tone.

'Your people? What people? We're just descendants, Jarrod. Aborigines were our ancestors. We're not them. Sure, we've got a bit of color in us but, you know … Look, we were going to ask if you want to stay with us for a while. I could clean out the guitar room.'

He sculled the rest of his beer. 'I feel sorry for you,' he said, with what seemed like real pity. 'Descendants? Really?'

I said nothing, until he rolled and then lit up his second smoke.

'So, you don't want to stay?'

'Of course not. I just wanted to tell you what I thought,' he answered. 'To get it off my chest.'

'Well, are you staying tonight? You can have Seth's bed. He can sleep with us.'

'The couch is fine, thanks. It's what I'm used to.'

~

I was in town a few weeks later. Susan had been pestering me to take Seth to the barbers, to replace his curls with a short back and sides. A bitter southerly, straight from Antarctica, was singing down Charles Street, sweeping frost-burned oak leaves into unruly mounds. We pushed head-first into the wind, following the spiked iron fence surrounding The Square, past the Aboriginal housing co-op and the small cafes with their alfresco tables. I could have gone the other way — the shorter way — but I wanted to walk through the park.

The Square was almost devoid of people in this bitter weather. A lone council worker in an orange hi-vis shirt rose from the bed of pink-and-white snapdragons he had been tending. I marveled at how something so beautiful and exotic could thrive in such bleak conditions. Seth watched the man push his wheelbarrow to the next bed, while I surveyed the rest of the park.

I crossed The Square, past the fountain, with Seth huddled against me. By the camellia border, on the far side, the parkies were bent over a small fire. Fires were banned in the park, but the council workers turn a blind eye in winter. They had one of their own, smouldering away by their quarters.

A gruff voice rose from the huddle as we approached, and the parkies shuffled and twisted, in some sort of acknowledgement. Seeing that my brother wasn't amongst them, I turned and headed back toward the fountain.

'Who are they, Daddy?' Seth was looking back at the parkies.

'*Our people*, apparently,' I said.

'Are we still going to the hair-cutters?'

A stiff gust drew a tear across my cheek, leaving a cold trail. I ran my fingers through Seth's thick, dark hair and walked him back the way we came, back to the car.

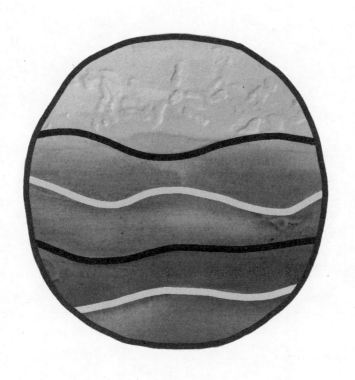

TIME AND TIDE

As the heavily laden tinnie turned and rode a wave into the small bay, James Beeton placed a hand on his son's shoulder and give it a sharp squeeze. He let go of the tiller while he took the brown sherry bottle from between his knees and the boat lurched forward on its own wake.

'Gunna be a good season,' he said, pointing the bottle toward their patch of muttonbird rookery along the coast of Big Dog Island. To his son, Henry, it sounded like an affirmation.

In the dying light and with the boat nosed against the shore, James passed a loaded cardboard box to Henry. A small shore-breaker jerked the bow skyward just enough to fling the box from Henry's grasp before he could fully take hold. The contents landed in the cold sea that rose and fell around his bare thighs.

'Shit, boy,' growled his dad. 'That's our only box of tucker. Grab what you can. Quick.'

Henry didn't answer. He was already snatching at packets of two-minute noodles that were holding their own in the water. Each one he rescued was folded into the crease of his t-shirt. He ran up the beach a way and dumped them on the sand. He was stripped down to his undies and the skin on his legs was reddened and tight.

On his way back into the water, he spied the treat that his mother had put in for him: the only treat they could afford this year. The block of Cadbury chocolate bobbed around the front of the tinnie. Not flat on the surface like the noodles but up-ended and half submerged; tragic yet glorious, like the sinking *Titanic*.

'Leave it,' said James. He had braced himself up the front of the tinnie, legs bent and on the lookout for the next waves. He took another pull on his bottle of plonk. 'Time and tide, boy. Go for the spuds. Don't lose the bloody spuds.'

Henry waded up to his neck, to where the vegetables were now floating. He lobbed them, one by one, high onto the beach. Now that the onions and the potatoes dotted the granite sand — between the wash and the two-foot-high pile of ribbon weed that ran the length of it — Henry went for his treat. His father had his head down, fussing with the ropes and preparing to tie up the boat. As Henry stooped for the chocolate, the boat pitched forward, knocking him beneath the bow.

Before he went under, Henry heard the grating, metallic thud and clank of heavy chain as James fell to the aluminum plate floor. The front of the boat pressed down on Henry, pinning him to the sand. He released his breath and inhaled just as the tide surged out. Before he could call for help, the next wave came over him and he was submerged once more. There was not enough water in the wave to lift the boat and release him. All he could do was hold his breath and wait.

There was a moment of serenity as the movement of the sea seemed to stall. Through the ripples, Henry could see the bright blue moon against a scarlet sky. Then a wavy shadow blocked out the moon and a long-necked bottle splashed into the water above. Its inky contents pulsed into the seawater in lazy gushes. At the end of his breath, Henry's heartbeat quickened. He screamed his last air into the sea as the cloud of black sherry enveloped him.

Henry came to between his father's legs. He was slumped forward and a projection of hot spit and mucus covered his groin — a string of it still hung from his bottom lip. There were drag marks in the sand that led up the beach, from the water's edge to the soles of his feet. Henry could smell his father's sweet breath as he silently sobbed against Henry's back. The only movement Henry dared make was to sneak the chocolate bar still gripped in his hand inside his shirt.

'Thought I'd lost you, boy,' his dad said, once he had gathered himself.

'I'm ... okay ... Dad,' Henry replied between coughs.

James got to his feet, anger rising in his voice. 'Fucken told you to leave it, didn't I?' He cuffed Henry on the side of the head, hard.

Henry rolled into a ball, covering himself.

After a while he cautiously lifted his head, his ear hot and throbbing, and watched his father load up with gear and trudge through the squeaking sand toward their sheds. But not before he opened a new bottle and took a long swig.

~

Henry and James spent the next day cleaning up the sheds. Over a breakfast of fried devon and baked beans, they had agreed on the division of tasks. It felt like a ritual and they barely spoke. James worked hard and fast, and Henry knew to keep out of his way. It didn't take long — they had done the same thing for as far back as Henry could remember.

The processing shed sat just above the beach. It was modern, unlike their quarters, which were old and run-down. The lease had been in Henry's family ever since his great-grandmother won it from a drunken shed-boss, in a card game at the end of one muttonbird season. Over the following years, people had patched up the accommodation and built on many times. During the last few seasons, Henry had observed the progression of the New Zealand spinach vine smothering the exterior — its tendrils invading the shed through openings large and small. It now looked like an eco-village someone might pay a fortune to stay in — until they looked inside.

~

In the afternoon, when the boat was afloat on the high tide, they went back to the main island to collect fuel to run their generator. Henry always marveled at their trusty Lister Petter. During birding, it was central to the whole show: lights in the bunkhouse and cookhouse, and power to run the cool room and water pump in the processing shed. The generator was their economy and diesel was its currency.

At the general store, Henry watched his father squint into his empty wallet for a moment after he'd paid the shopkeeper for the fuel. Out in the car park, James stopped and looked out across Franklin Sound to Big Dog Island, their island, his chiseled jaw set in defiance.

'This should get us through the season,' said James. Henry knew the statement was not to him, but a challenge to the gods.

It was the same every year. His father put it all on the line for birding. And with each year that passed, the stress of it never waned. But the pay-off was worth it. After the harvest — after the birds were sold — they made enough money to scrape through the year.

Henry smiled to himself as they bumped back over to Big Dog Island. He was at the tiller this time, his father weighing down the bow as they cut into the wind. If all went well,

Henry's take this year would be two grand. He had already put a small, non-refundable holding payment on a road bike that he had spent all year dreaming about buying. A bike and a learner's license equalled freedom in Henry's mind.

They worked on into the night so that they could start birding the following day. The Lister Petter provided the soundtrack to their birding trips: a ceaseless drone from daybreak to dark, raising and lowering in octave with the variation of its load. One of his dad's sayings was, 'You've never known silence like a generator switched off.'

~

'Got a bird yet?' James called, from across the track.

They'd set off before dawn to work a patch up on the hill.

'No, you?' Henry answered. The tussocks were sparse in this part of their lease, and Henry could see clearly where the old birds had been moving around and scratching at their holes. This was their go-to spot, early in the season, and they always did well here. He sat up in the rookery. The tussocks parted and waved in the place where his father's voice came from.

'Not a damned thing.'

'Think someone's been here already?' asked Henry. He gave up trying, having been down at least fifty good holes. All he'd pulled up was one angry old bird that had squawked at him while it tore at his wrists with its scaly feet.

'Dunno. You can't trust half the black bastards on this island, can ya? We'll go and have a look down Old Snakey, ay?'

They met back on the track, spits in hand, and looked each other up and down for a second. James was a solid man, but sinewy. He had strong, masculine features and a grim, determined look about him. A difficult look to warm to. Henry often wondered what his mother saw in him. Standing there with a ripped tea towel over his head like a bandana, short fingerless gloves and a three-day beard, his father resembled a militia fighter from one of the war-torn countries regularly on the news. Henry doubted he appeared much different, except he was taller and lanky and carried a light layer of what his father teasingly called 'puppy fat' on his face. He'd shed it one day.

Old Snakey was a section of track at the bottom of their rookery, close to their shed. Growing up, Henry assumed it was called that because it was a winding part of the track. He later learned that it was because birders often saw snakes in that area — mostly whip snakes but also the odd tiger.

Finding a good section of rookery each, they drove their spits into the ground and started working the holes.

After a while, James held up a scrawny chick. It barely had enough energy to scratch at him. 'One bird — not even a keeper.'

They worked the patch until the sun had dried out the dew on the ground. They only pulled out two more birds that were of size (and even then only just). It had taken nearly two hours to get those. They sat and ate their smoko on the edge of the track. Afterward they lay back in the rookery, where it smelled like dry straw and game. James made up a rollie and smoked it while Henry sucked on the single square of chocolate he'd brought along. He'd decided to ration himself to one per day.

Henry was the first to speak. 'What's going on, Dad?'

'Fucked if I know, boy.'

~

They'd called it quits before lunch and walked back to their shed in silence. Even though it had been swept out and cleaned inside, the sharp smell of mice hit Henry's nose like vinegar. James sat at the table, sipped cold tea and rolled cigarettes until he had a small pile. Some of the flex had left his jaw, and Henry thought he looked older and slightly softer, somehow.

James scooped the rollies into an empty White Ox packet and stuffed them in his top pocket. 'Going next door to see what's up with these birds,' he said. He snatched a brown bottle from the driftwood shelf above the oven, where there was still a full crate of whisky, and kicked open the flyscreen door.

~

From the bunkhouse window, Henry watched his father walk up the track. It took at least fifteen minutes to reach the next shed around the point. The bunkhouse he shared with his father was cosy. It had a long window made of a car windscreen built into the wall. Green light filtered through the vine-covered glass. The wall with the window was clad in corrugated iron, so during the day the room was warm and dry. The other walls were lined with rough-sawn timber and plastered with yellowing newspaper.

Henry lay down on his bed and lowered his trousers. He could count on one hand the number of times he had been left at the shed by himself, over his entire life. Usually, his mother was there and — before the accident — his little sister, Lucy, was always at his heels.

Henry slid his hand into his undies and took hold of himself. Stuck on the wall next to his head was a Kmart lingerie advertisement featuring a woman posing in vintage underwear. Henry had grown up with her, but over the last few years he'd come to like the way she stared at him. That knowing look. It wasn't Henry's routine to jerk off with his eyes open, but every time he shut them, the scene from the previous afternoon was before him: pinned down by the boat, the dizzying sensation as he ran out of breath. The blackness. He took a long time to finish, and was so exhausted when he did that he fell asleep with his pants still down.

It was late afternoon when Henry woke. And it was quiet, which meant his father had still not returned. He refueled the generator and, on the beach, he cleaned the two birds they'd caught earlier. He stewed the birds with some potatoes and onions and seasoned the stew with whatever he could find in the metal cupboard by the sink. The cupboard was full of rusty cans with no labels — 'surprise bags,' his father called them.

Henry checked the internet on his phone and was pleased to find he had a few bars of reception. He googled 'muttonbirds' and scrolled through the results, searching for an article he had found before the season, about dead muttonbirds washing up on a beach near Sydney. The scientists had predicted a poor breeding season and blamed climate change. They said the birds' food was scarce due to rising ocean temperatures. Climate change. Henry didn't show it to James when he finally returned. His father didn't believe in climate change — or the internet.

~

The next morning James sat at the fold-up table with his rough head in his rough hands, staring at the plate in front of him. Henry had cracked open a 'surprise bag' for breakfast, which turned out to be spaghetti. He fried it in a pan with slices of devon.

James eventually lifted his head and poked at his food with a shaking hand. 'The Watsons are packing up. Going home.'

'Really?'

'No birds.'

Henry had a strong urge to tell his dad about the muttonbird article but decided against it. He mustered the courage to ask the question that had been waiting in his mouth. 'What are we going to do then?'

James shrugged and squinted at the shelf holding all the alcohol. His tongue dapped at the corner of his thin, dry lips.

~

'I'll give you two hundred for it,' said Old Man Bligh, still sitting on his tractor out the front of the Beetons' shed. The Fergie 35 burbled away without missing a beat. Henry had often wondered what sort of strange power the older white men of the islands wielded to keep such ancient gear running. Old Man Bligh had a lease on the far side of the island — one that existed before the island was returned to Aboriginal ownership.

'That's over seven hundred bucks' worth of diesel there,' said James. He rapped on the top of each drum to prove they were full.

'Maybe, but I'm offering two hundred.'

There was a gap in the conversation while they eyed each other off.

'Listen,' said James, shoving his hands in his pockets and exhaling slowly. 'You know there's no birds. I just need to get me and the boy home. Just a bit more … please.'

From his place high up on the tractor, Old Man Bligh looked across at Henry, who was leaning against the shed. He gave a gap-toothed smile and crossed his arms over his huge, sweating belly.

'Two hundred,' he repeated.

'Fuck off, then,' yelled James, holding up a shaking fist, index finger extended. The cords in his neck were straining.

A ball of thick, soot-filled smoke cannoned from the tractor's exhaust as Old Man Bligh put his foot down and ground the 35 into gear.

'Maggot. Got no right to be here, anyway!'

Old Man Bligh took off up the track, bouncing as he hit the tussock butts at speed. Henry knew better than to get in his father's way and stood back as James ran to the corner of the shed, where a broken aluminum cooking pot lay, strangled by kikuyu grass. He ripped the pot free, took a short run-up and threw it after the tractor. It tumbled through the air awkwardly but somehow found its mark. When the pot hit the back of Old Man Bligh's bald head, it resounded like a gong, and the tractor lurched forward. James stared after the tractor, waiting for the driver to fall, but it kept going, disappearing round the bends of Old Snakey.

'Rogue,' said James, then rested his hands on his knees and leaned forward to breathe deeply.

'*Dong!*' said Henry, mimicking the sound of the pot.

James fell onto his back, face contorted. Alarmed, Henry leaped to his side. When he realized his father was laughing, Henry started too. And they lay on the edge of the track until their laughter died, and watched the adult birds come whistling in from the sea, bringing the night-time with them.

~

Henry didn't hear his dad leave the following morning. There was a note on the table. *Important business. Back later. Start packing up.*

The shelf where his father kept his grog was bare. Henry knew this meant he would be drinking somewhere at one of the other sheds and wouldn't be home until dark — if at all. He made a mental note to be in bed early. Taking a cup of tea back with him to bed, Henry almost slipped on a motorcycle maga-zine on the floor. His dream of getting the road bike he wanted, the freedom he yearned for, was now gone. *Why were there no birds?* He kicked the magazine across the room. It fanned out and knocked a white candle, set into an abalone shell, from the small table next to his father's bed. Henry quickly reattached the candle with melted wax.

His dad's suede shaving bag was also on his bedside table. Henry had a strong urge to look inside. It smelled of mint and bar soap. James used a straight razor. It had a bone handle and reminded Henry of the old-fashioned butter knives he'd found in the drawers of his grandfather's garage — lying amongst vin-tage spark-plug tins full of assorted screws, bobbins of copper wire and dirty knobs of wax. He unfolded the razor. The blade was dull and scratched, showing its age. But he knew it would be extremely sharp — his father wasn't the sort of man to keep a blunt razor. He placed the sharp edge against the pale, almost translucent part of his wrist and drew it upward, slowly, like they did in the movies.

The small hairs from the inside of his arm floated silently to the floor.

Next to the razor was a white pill bottle. His father's name was on the newly printed sticker, alongside *Valium, 5 mg.* Henry had started noticing the pill bottles the year before. His mother, too, had her own stash: one in her bedside drawer at home, and another in her handbag. Henry could tell from a shake that it was full. He applied pressure to the cap and twisted. With his sweet tea he swallowed two pills. He had been meaning to try the drug that had waltzed his parents through the dark ballroom after his little sister's death. Now seemed the perfect time.

~

The processing shed didn't need scrubbing as it hadn't even been used. Henry packed all the birding equipment — fish bins, stools, the gas ring-burner for the scalding pot, hessian bags, opening knives and more — into the cool room, where it would store for another year. The Valium calmed Henry. It did a much better job than warm milk ever could. He got on with his work with a clear head, no longer concerned about his father — how drunk he would be later, how he was going to get them home. He even put aside his grief about the road bike and the deposit he would lose. The thoughts were still there of course, but the Valium smoothed them over somehow.

With the bulk of the work done, Henry went back to their quarters. Without really thinking about it, he took his father's pills and his block of chocolate and went walking. This was the first time he had left their lease since he had been on the island this season. He went north on Old Snakey. The pot that had hit Old Man Bligh still lay off to the side of the track amongst a bunch of paper daisies. He used to walk a lot with his mother and Lucy, especially of a Sunday, when they had the day off. Nobody worked on a Sunday. They were good times — even with his father around. When Lucy was small and couldn't see above the tussocks, Henry would describe the surroundings to her, like you would to a blind person. Sometimes he would describe things that weren't there, fanciful things, and she would amble along behind, eyes half closed. *Tell me again, Henry,* she would say. *Again.* And Henry would, many times over.

Henry found himself taking the track that led to Rileys Point. He unwrapped the chocolate and ate it in large, satisfying mouthfuls until it was finished. The track was long and straight but dipped down at the end, where it reached the coast. It was just off this point that the accident had happened, and Henry hadn't been back since. The sea was choppy that day — there was not a large swell. Any other day, the wave that swamped the boat would have barely been a bump. But the tinnie was so overloaded with people and gear that the bow couldn't even rise. A rope had dragged Lucy down with the boat as it sank, life jacket and all. She had just learned to swim but didn't get the chance to test her skills in the water with Henry and her parents.

As he approached the end of the track, Henry tipped all the pills into his hand. Where the bank met the sea, there was a craggy basalt cave. Creeper vine hung down over the entrance of the cave, and the surrounding foreshore was carpeted in kanikung. Henry and Lucy used to play here, in their secret grotto. On crisp mornings at the end of the birding season, they would lie here while the young birds — the lucky ones that didn't end up as part of the harvest — would waddle around them on their journey to the shore. Here, their instincts would kick in, and they'd flap and squawk and blink into the new day's light, as if urging each other on. As the chicks reached the water, Henry would shield Lucy's eyes and sing into her ear as the mollyhawks and the crows swooped on the weaker ones and pecked out their eyes.

Coming to the end of the track, and with his face wet with tears, Henry brought the handful of pills up to his mouth. But something wasn't right — someone was here. Henry stopped and stood, motionless, until he realized who it was. His dad stood in front of a large wooden cross and was carving something into it. Henry flung the pills into the rookery and wiped his eyes and face with his sleeve. He approached the cross. Some of his father's tools were scattered on the ground and an empty bag of pre-mixed cement was weighed down by a rock. James didn't seem surprised to see his son.

'R.I.P. Lucy Beeton,' read Henry, out loud.

His father turned to him. The pride seemed to have returned to his face, his jaw once again set in defiance. 'We're going home tomorrow, boy,' he said.

'Really?' replied Henry. 'Sold the diesel?'

His father didn't answer. Didn't need to. Henry couldn't see the box of whisky anywhere. And his dad, when he accompanied Henry back up the track, was steady on his feet.

KITE

The kite, dangling from the ceiling of my kombi, caught my eye for the second time that afternoon. I studied it with guilt. The kite was unused, barely even thought about. A Christmas gift from my nephew, Connor, who the family just call 'Boy.'

My sister sent Boy to a Steiner school, much to the annoyance of our Nanna, who was convinced it would put him at a disadvantage.

'No grandson of mine will be living in the long grass,' she said, when my sister told her about the school. 'Put him in the state school, so he can piss next to the rich kids.'

But the Steiner school worked out well for Boy, who had always been a hands-on kid. A month earlier, at Christmas dinner at Nanna's, he'd presented me with the flat, diamond-shaped object, wrapped in newspaper. I could tell it was something homemade, even before I opened it. And the way he tucked his long fringe behind his ear, concealing his smile through a closed mouth — all of that showed that the gift was something he was proud of.

Before I'd removed the last of the wrapping, he started on the explanation.

'It's practically unbreakable,' he said, taking it away from me. He tapped at the wooden struts of the kite with his fingernails. 'My own design, Unc. I found the straightest blackwood branches I could and spent days scraping them with a rock and hardening them in the fire — like how we hone a spear, you know? Listen, they're like steel.' He tapped again at the wood and it did, indeed, sound dense and hard.

I admired the kite, although I felt it was a strange gift for an adult. It was well constructed, the fabric stretched taut across the frame, and it was in the colors of the Aboriginal flag, with the sun at its center.

'The center pole sticks out further than normal kites. That's the unique design. The other kites I made all snapped when they hit the ground. But this one is strong.'

I didn't doubt him for a second. The middle stick protruded a handspan beyond the top of the kite and was sharpened to a point.

'We should give her a run,' I said, mostly for his sake. I couldn't deny, though, that the prospect of reliving my childhood — if only fleetingly — was attractive.

'No wind, Unc,' he said, looking out the window. 'But I've already given her a razz, and phew' — he made a whistling sound and his face opened into a grin, full of straight, white teeth — 'she's deadly.'

~

The van had been my home for the last seven months. It was meant to be a sabbatical, from time served in a job that had sculpted frown lines in my forehead deep enough to make Michelangelo proud. I'd hoped a minimalist adventure would be the new botox. But the rear-view mirror didn't show much of a change — perhaps it was just too early to tell.

I swirled the dregs of coffee around my tin mug and flung it out the door of the van. It blew back in, speckling my shorts and my shirt. A wind had picked up. My nephew's kite twisted and jigged against the ceiling with sudden life. It reminded me of that early Frankenstein film, when the inanimate body jolts with electricity and spasms into being.

I'd lazed in the van all day and my bones were getting sore. And now a steady wind was blowing across the bluff. It made sense to try out the kite. If for no other reason than to avoid a lie, next time I spoke to Boy about his gift. He'd be asking, no doubt about it.

~

There was something different about this day, setting it apart from every other day in the van. It was a public holiday.

Australia Day.

The car park overlooking the bluff was packed. There were at least six parked vehicles parading small plastic Australian flags either side of their front windscreens, like they belonged to the Prime Minister's motorcade. I took the treated pine boardwalk that dissected the boobialla foreshore and made my way onto the beach. The wind almost snatched the kite from my hand.

Taking in the view, I observed two seas: a bright-green one with foamy waves and hovering seagulls; and one of red, white and blue. Now, I'm not a political person. I don't care much about what our mob call 'Invasion Day.' But I'll admit, I was intimidated.

If it wasn't for the wind tugging at Boy's kite — the beckoning thrum of energy flowing through the short length of string I had unwound — I might have turned back. Returned to the van and found something else to do.

Perhaps I should have. There were people everywhere.

I looked behind me. There were groups scattered across the open grassed area above the beach. Most were on picnic blankets, some with umbrellas. Others had flimsy Kmart pop-up tents. Small kids were riding small bikes with orange flags attached on tall, whippy stems. They were learning that riding on the grass is hard as hell. Under art-deco barbecue awnings, extended families sprawled in the shade. Their faces were smug and their movements languid, indicating to the scouting new-comers like me that they wouldn't be moving on anytime soon. They had Australian flag-decorated Eskys and held stubby cool-ers in tattooed hands.

Now, as I walked onto the beach, it was faces that wore the colors. The sale of colored zinc cream must be a goldmine for the local shops and pharmacies over this weekend. It was everywhere — smeared across countenances like white peo-ple's ocher.

I've always felt the beach was a neutral place: a demilitarized zone. A place where it is acceptable to smile at fellow revelers, kick a ball back to its owner, or run crazy and childlike into the sea. A place devoid of judgement. We are drawn to the beach, it seems, to that fuzzy boundary at the edge of our world. We're just like the tide, in that way. And I often wonder what force it is that pulls us. My family say it's because we're saltwater people, but I'm almost certain that most humans feel it.

~

The distance between the foreshore and the water — a long way out, this afternoon — felt like a walk of shame. Me with my rustic kite of black, yellow and red, standing out against the backdrop of Aussie patriotism.

I was keenly aware that every eye was on me and I caught unfavorable comments about my presence on snatches of breeze. The mood was heightened because an Aboriginal guy burned the Australian flag at a 'Change The Date' rally earlier in the day in Hobart. It was all over the news. He martyred himself, this guy, and now he was loved and hated alike. Already, on the radio, a local politician was calling for changes to the law, making them retrospective, so that the guy who burned the flag could be heavily fined or imprisoned. I was trying not to think about it too much — thoughts like that are no good for the frown.

I passed a large family group who had set up on the beach. They had a white poodle that yapped at me. They held it back but made no move to silence it. I avoided eye contact, but I couldn't miss seeing nine Australian flag camp chairs, another colored Esky, and two red, white and blue umbrellas. They were rowdy, this crowd — like they'd been drinking steadily all day. Some of the group were setting up beach cricket on the hard, rippled surface of the flats. I veered slightly away from them, toward a patch of clear, wet sand near the water.

Flick, flick went the metallic clink of flint against steel, unmistakable behind me.

'Yeah, fuck off with your Abo flag,' came an assured voice. And I felt fear. Not because of the threat — I'd been bracing myself for that — but because the voice belonged to a woman.

~

I laid the kite on the sand and the front lifted and fell a few times before a gust gave it enough loft to catch the breeze. It pulled, hard, and the more line I released, the more I felt the power of the wind. I found myself bracing my feet in the sand, feeling the weight and sturdiness of the kite. It wasn't like the balsa wood and supermarket bag kites we made as kids. This felt like there was something alive at the end of my line. It felt like a game fish, thrashing and struggling, angry and inconsolable in its plight.

Boy had wound the long string onto a clap-stick, taken from a set he had no doubt crafted himself. Its smooth finish allowed it to spin freely through my fingers as the kite surged to the heavens. It was the highest thing in the sky.

Some way down the beach, a man helped a young girl launch a plastic Aussie flag kite. It zigzagged for a while before the string snapped and it floated out over the sea. The child dropped to her knees and threw the handle at her father before pounding her fists into the sand. The man looked around, embarrassed. The frayed, white string trailed below the kite as the wind whipped it well out past the breakers, like a horse loose at the reins.

Meanwhile, beach walkers stopped to watch my kite. They appeared oblivious to its colors and just seemed to be admiring its movements and its height. I beamed like Boy had when he gave it to me. I was proud of him. My nephew.

The wind was coming in strongly from the south but every now and again it would drop out slightly and the line would go lax, sending the kite into a steep dive toward the ocean. And as the wind picked up again, the descent would speed up. It reminded me of the muttonbirds coming back to their burrows of an evening — little dive-bombers, built for speed, not accuracy. Then, with a jerk of my wrist, the kite would turn, and its velocity would send it back into the sky, wowing my spectators, and me as well. This went on for a good half-hour.

~

Finally, the wind began to lessen, and the kite lost its vigor. Some of the observers turned away in disappointment. With the spell of the kite broken, all that was left were the colors overhead, weakly descending in a side-to-side motion. I sensed the mood change, and I heard someone use the word *divisive*.

With regret in my heart, I wound the kite in. It came back to me with little resistance. When it was maybe forty meters out, something happened. The wind changed direction and picked up speed once more. The kite darted horizontally across the sky with new resolve and then held into the wind above the large family on the beach — the ones I'd passed on my way down. Out of my control, and as if to show off, the kite darted one way and then another as the wind gusts battled overhead.

One of the beach cricketers lobbed on to a good one and the wet tennis ball drove toward the family. The poodle set off after the ball and took it up in its mouth. Thinking it was a game, the poodle ran with the ball along the beach, with the children and some of the adults in tow.

A gust sent Boy's kite up vertically and it flipped over and dive-bombed again. But this time, as I flicked my wrist and tugged at the string, the kite did not respond.

The kite met the dog at the water's edge and impaled it into the sand. It didn't make a sound, but its back legs tried to keep running. One of the young cricketers was clotheslined by the string that had the injured poodle and what was left of Boy's kite on one end, and me on the other. The child was whipped back into the sand, shocked but unhurt.

A bystander pushed me down before I could resist, and another pinned me to the ground.

I didn't struggle.

'You're not going anywhere, buddy,' someone said.

'Not until the police arrive,' added another.

On the radio, they'd said that the name of that guy — the one who burned the Australian flag — would be mud, after what he did. But I knew that to many — including my nephew, Boy — he'd be a hero. But what, I wondered, would they say about a man who, on Australia Day, speared a white dog?

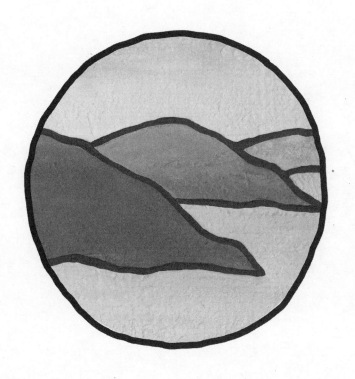

MORPORK

It all started when I discovered that my brother was sleeping with my wife. It was a Saturday and I was rostered on to work. My boss had asked me to run some errands in town before heading out to the job site. We were working with a volunteer conservation group, planting trees along rivers. I was semi-retired, following a career as an accountant. This was a lifestyle job and it gave me something to do. Something outside.

It was late September — well and truly into spring — a bright, clear day, heightened somehow by vivid greens and blues in my vision. It must have been some sort of unique combination of weather and my body's chemistry but, somehow, I was back in my childhood. For a few magic moments I just stood in the sun, on the footpath outside the Launceston mall, taking it all in, knowing that I only had a short time to savor the experience. It was an intoxicating sensory reunion: the smell of the paints I used in kindergarten, a song often heard while I was still learning to walk. Most of the memories were whisked away as quickly as they surfaced. But a few I managed to hold on to and keep, like fragments of a welcome, erotic dream.

When the memories subsided, and still in a quiet daze, I happened to glance down a narrow alley that led to my favorite restaurant: The Aristocrat. The place I'd proposed to Cindy. At the entrance, partially concealed by the shade of the striped awning, I saw a woman and a man locked in an embrace. The man had his back to me, but the woman's head was thrown back, her eyes closed, lips pressed in an involuntary smile. It wasn't the fact that my wife was with another man that wrung my heart out like a sponge. It was the look of passion on her face. A look I hadn't seen for a long, long time — perhaps over thirty years. And the fact that I knew immediately, from the bold and confident stance and the olive hand intertwined with hers, that the man was my brother.

Rex. Fifteen years my junior, cocky and swaggering. We had always been miles apart. But as the couple separated — their identities now fully confirmed — I had the realization that you can have a brother who is not a brother at all.

I hid myself from view as they walked out of the alley. Out in the open, they became strangers, melting into the lines of bodies streaming along the footpath. The shock of discovery, of finding them together, along with that strange childhood flashback, made it all seem like a dream. I could have happily convinced myself it wasn't real at all.

~

Following this encounter, Cindy's love for me didn't seem to change, at least not on the surface. She continued to use my pet name, rubbed my shoulders while I watched the evening news, and went to sleep cuddling my arm every night. And I didn't see Rex any more than usual, which was only a few times a year. But when he did come around, there *was* something there — something I perhaps wouldn't have noticed had I not known about them. Cindy always placed him next to her at the dinner table and their hands would dip under the table several times over the course of the evening. Rex would agree with the things Cindy said, which was unusual as Rex was a real lefty, while Cindy was more conservative. It all added up, yet I couldn't understand it.

Cindy and I were in our fifties. We spent our spare time gardening, our weekends cruising the Tamar River with our yacht-club friends. Rex was the CEO of an Aboriginal organization, often out on the town using his profile and reputation to pull younger women. He was a player through and through. So what was he doing with my wife?

I became so consumed by their relationship that I struggled to concentrate on everyday tasks, and I couldn't handle being in the house with Cindy. I began camping out by the rivers where we were planting the trees, telling Cindy it was a temporary requirement of the job.

It was around that time that I began to fantasize about the satisfaction I would feel if Rex were to die. And, particularly, if he were to die by my hand.

I'm not a violent man, so the conventional methods I knew of were completely off the table. And I wanted Cindy to feel the pain of his death too — I longed to see her suffering in solitude, like I had been.

The idea came to me the morning I heard the morpork. It had been a cold night on the river, and I had gone to sleep early. I woke about three in the morning, to the wail of an owl in the blackwood tree overhanging my tent.

Morpork, morpork.

The story of the morpork was one of the memories that returned the day I discovered Cindy and Rex together. I was back in my great-grandmother's red-brick unit, on the old back road out of Beaconsfield. I must have been about six or seven; she in her mid-eighties. Earlier we'd made toffee apples and I'd eaten mine in front of the radiator while we played Memory with a deck of cards. I was sitting on the bed, still sucking the sugar from my teeth, when Nan came out of the bathroom in a paisley nightdress. I always slept next to her — that's how it was done in our family.

'I s'pose you want a story, boy.'

I didn't but I couldn't say no.

We got into bed and she yanked the long, dirty string on the ceiling lamp. It was so dark in the room I could see fuzzy flashing shapes in my vision. The room, like my great-grandmother, smelled of mothballs.

We lay there for a while before she began to speak. Her voice was shrill.

'When I was a little girl, there was a man who lived by himself in a tiny hut at the back of our place. Real dark fella, he was. Way darker 'n us. Old Tom, we called him. Old Tom had a horse named Piney. You still awake, boy?'

'Yes, Nan.'

'Good. Mum and Da used to make me stop with Old Tom when they went off to town. Took a long time, back then, to get from Pine Scrub to Whitemark. Course that was before there were motor cars. They used to use Piney to help carry the supplies back. Be a good day in and a good day back in them days, and that was if Da didn't get on the drink and go playin' up.

'Now, some people thought Old Tom was a bit strange, and Mum didn't like leavin' me there. But Da didn't like what people said about the ol' fella. Old Tom had been to the war, see. One night, as Old Tom was pokin' the fire, we heard the morpork outside the hut ... *Morpork* ... *Morpork*.'

When my great-grandmother made the sound of the owl, her voice raised an octave. It cracked and sounded insane.

'"That's the third night in a row the morpork's been around," Old Tom said. Poor old fella's skin had gone grey. "You know what that means, don't you, my girl? Means me days are numbered."

'Mum and Da returned the next afternoon. By then, I'd forgotten about what Old Tom had said about the morpork. But, that night, Old Tom's hut caught alight. Da reckoned it musta been a log rolled from the fire. And we could 'ear him wailin' and wailin' in there too. Trapped, like.'

My great-grandmother was silent for a while. I was clinging to the bed, frightened. It didn't help if I closed my eyes or not; the scene lingered there in the dark.

'Let this be a lesson to ya, my boy. The morpork is the bringer of death. If you hear it callin' to ya — *morpork … morpork* — three nights in a row, means ya gonna die. Now, git to bloody sleep.'

~

I needed to catch this morpork. Before I attempted it, I called Rex to find out when he would be away next, using the pretense of wanting to borrow his lawnmower. He told me he would be in Melbourne the following weekend.

Luckily, the morpork at my camp came back the next night. I listened to it make its sound until the sun came up. I had to catch it before the next evening or risk hearing it for a third night in a row. At daybreak, the morpork flew to a tree about forty meters from the river and flitted into a hollow halfway up the trunk.

At lunch I told the boss I wasn't feeling well and went back to my camp. I scaled the tree and found the morpork asleep in the hollow, surrounded by the delicate bones of small creatures. It tore at my forearms when I seized it and tried to slip a small rubber band over its beak. Its bright, circled eyes and disapproving frown bore into my soul, seeing the pathetic man I had become — the man Cindy and Rex had created.

It rode next to me in the car, its body wrapped in my pillowcase and only its head sticking out. The rubber band effectively suppressed its call. A teenage boy served me at the pet shop where I bought a cage and birdseed. He eyed the weeping furrows in the skin of my forearms and the streaks of blood on my shirt.

Once home, I put the bird in the cage with a matchbox full of birdseed and left it in the back seat of my car with the pillowcase draped over it.

Cindy was happy to see me after the few days I'd been away. I cuddled her from behind as she washed the dishes, then we made love with her leaning into the sink. Afterward we held hands on the couch and watched TV. It was the most intimate we had been for years, but I couldn't stop thinking about the morpork out in the car.

It wasn't hard to find Rex's spare house key; it was inside a fake rock next to a potted yucca at his front door. Rex's house was modern — everything about him was modern. With a high-paying job and no family, he had money for new things. I found the manhole above Rex's laundry and grabbed the ladder from the internal garage, then I carried the morpork up into the roof space.

When I took the pillowcase off the cage, the morpork swiveled to look at me. Its head had a disturbing amount of range, and its yellow, unblinking eyes glowed like they were lit from the inside. Much about this bird seemed unnatural. It hadn't eaten the birdseed, now spilled across the bottom of the cage, and I realized why: it was a carnivore, and its beak had been fastened shut anyway. I shone my phone torch across the sea of insulation and was satisfied from the scatters of mouse droppings that the morpork would find its own food. When I opened the cage, it moved to the entrance, like it knew it had a job to do. It let me remove the rubber band from its beak. After a moment it flew from the cage and landed on one of the roof trusses, where it perched, silent. It didn't look at me again.

I packed the ladder away and put the key back in the fake rock. Rex would never know I had been inside. I took his lawnmower from the shed and put it in the car. Before I left, I stood for a few minutes with my head cocked. It was a still, overcast morning, but there was no sound other than cars passing by.

~

Rex died a week later. Cindy took the call from the police, and her fingernails dug into my back as she held me afterward and sobbed through her words. I smiled to myself as she broke down. Massive heart attack, the police suspected, as Rex had died on the couch watching TV, his dinner half-eaten on his lap.

I waited for her to stop crying before I spoke. 'I know about you and Rex,' I said.

~

Cindy and I separated soon after. I let her keep the house, as Rex had left me his place — I was his only sibling. I made toffee apples on the first night I stayed there, and I sat on Rex's couch in the spot the police said he had died, thinking about the phone conversation I'd had with him the day before his death.

'I know this is a weird question, but did Nan ever tell you stories about an owl when you were a kid?'

'No,' I lied.

'She told them to me, but do you think I can remember how they went?'

'Why do you ask, Rex?'

'No reason,' he said.

I let the silence hang for a while before I spoke again.

'Don't pay any mind to those stories, Rex. Those old fellas *were* a superstitious lot.'

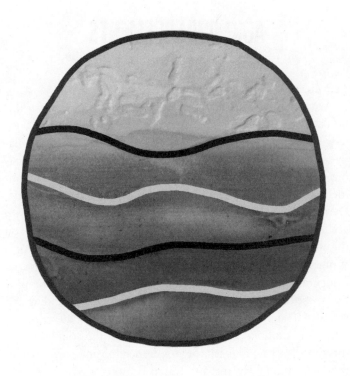

ACKNOWLEDGEMENTS

I am eternally thankful to the following:

Aviva Tuffield and the UQP team for having a vision for this book, and for whipping it into shape. The Wheeler Centre staff, judges and fellow recipients of the inaugural Next Chapter initiative — an amazing ride. The Aesop Foundation for your generous financial support. Cate Kennedy and Kate Gordon for your mentoring and friendship. I couldn't have done this without you. Denise Robinson for your encouragement and assistance with grants. Nathan Maynard and Aaron Everett for your feedback on the stories — and for just being brothers. Varuna, the National Writers' House and the Copyright Agency for awarding me an inaugural First Nations Fellowship and for providing the time and space to write. Arts Tasmania for your ongoing funding and support. The Tasmanian Aboriginal Centre for all the opportunities, and more importantly, being there for the community all this time. Michael Mansell for your leadership and dedication to the cause. Jimmy Everett and Karen Brown for paving the way with your stories and poetry. Melissa Lucashenko, Tony Birch, Ellen van Neerven, Tara June Winch and Bob Brown, for your generous and thoughtful endorsements. Everyone who showed an interest in my stories.

The Tasmanian Aboriginal people, past and present.

And to my grandparents, Elaine and Geoff Anderson, my brother Seth, and to Shenna and Sunni, for your patience and unconditional love.

The author would also like to thank the following publications where earlier versions of these stories were first published: 'Sonny' in *Griffith Review*, Edition 70: *Generosities of Spirit*, 2020. 'Honey' in *Kill Your Darlings*, 9 July 2018.

Two Dollar Radio
Books too loud to Ignore

ALSO AVAILABLE Here are some other titles you might want to dig into.

A HISTORY OF MY BRIEF BODY
ESSAYS BY BILLY-RAY BELCOURT

→ **Lambda Literary Award, Finalist.**

← "Stunning... Happiness, this beautiful book says, is the ultimate act of resistance." —Michelle Hart, *O, The Oprah Magazine*

A BRAVE, RAW, AND fiercely intelligent collection of essays and vignettes on grief, colonial violence, joy, love, and queerness.

ALLIGATOR STORIES BY DIMA ALZAYAT

→ **PEN/Robert W. Bingham Award for Debut Short Story Collection, longlist.**
→ **Swansea University Dylan Thomas Prize 2021, shortlist.**

← "A stellar debut... Alzayat manages to execute a short but thoughtful meditation on the spectrum of race in America from Jackson's presidency to present." —Colin Groundwater, *GQ*

THE AWARD-WINNING STORIES in Dima Alzayat's collection are luminous and tender, rich and relatable, chronicling a sense of displacement through everyday scenarios.

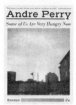

SOME OF US ARE VERY HUNGRY NOW
ESSAYS BY ANDRE PERRY

→ **Best Books 2019: *Pop Matters***
← "A complete, deep, satisfying read." —Gabino Iglesias, NPR

ANDRE PERRY'S DEBUT COLLECTION of personal essays travels from Washington DC to Iowa City to Hong Kong in search of both individual and national identity while displaying tenderness and a disarming honesty.

VIRTUOSO NOVEL BY YELENA MOSKOVICH

← "A bold feminist novel." —*Times Literary Supplement*

← "Told through multiple unique, compelling voices, the book's time and action are layered, with possibilities and paths forming rhythmic, syncopated interludes that emphasize that history is now." — Letitia Montgomery-Rodgers, *Foreword Reviews, starred review*

WITH A DISTINCTIVE PROSE FLAIR and spellbinding vision, a story of love, loss, and self-discovery that heralds Yelena Moskovich as a brilliant and one-of-a-kind visionary.

TRIANGULUM NOVEL BY MASANDE NTSHANGA

→ **2020 Nomo Awards Shortlist**
→ **A Best Book of 2019 —*LitReactor, Entropy***

← "Magnificently disorienting and meticulously constructed." —Tobias Carroll, Tor.com

AN AMBITIOUS, OFTEN PHILOSOPHICAL AND GENRE-BENDING NOVEL that covers a period of over 40 years in South Africa's recent past and near future.